W9-BWR-985

THE
PATCHWORK
MAN

Novels by David Harper

HIJACKED
BIG SATURDAY
THE GREEN AIR
THE PATCHWORK MAN

THE PATCHWORK MAN

David Harper

DODD, MEAD & COMPANY
New York

Library of Congress Cataloging in Publication Data

Harper, David.
  The patchwork man.

    I. Title.
PZ4.H292Pat   [PS3558.A62477]   813'.5'4   74–2474
ISBN 0–396–07135–X

This story is dedicated to a gentle man,
LARRY TURMAN

CONTENTS

Part One
ATLANTA

ONE

I AM not what I seem.

Empty your pockets.

Put everything on the table. Money, keys, nail clippers to one side. They don't count. Let me see the rest.

Driver's license.

Diner's Club card.

Blue Cross registration.

Social Security card.

A photograph of a pretty blonde woman hugging a young boy with mud on his face.

Is that all?

Be sure. Because these folded slips of paper, these plastic cards embossed with your name and identifying number, these tiny slices of remembrance captured in a Kodak color print, these *objects* are you, and they will accompany you from the day you are born until the day you die.

And, should the time come *before* you die, that you

3

must somehow cease to exist, this blizzard of paper-work—this chain of documented existence—must also cease to be.

Go ahead. Put a match to it.

You hesitate.

Why? Are you reluctant to give up your identity?

I understand. I was reluctant, too.

TWO

I NEVER really liked Atlanta. It is a sprawling patch of hasty construction and jumbled streets that sprouted beyond reason during the postwar boom and none of the old names have meaning any more. Peachtree Street is ribboned between greedy high-rise buildings and garish store fronts. The Automobile Club of America warns that only the eternal optimist hopes to find parking downtown, and the Club is correct. But if you insist on coming to Atlanta, there are worse places to begin your exploration than the Five Points intersection, where Marietta, Decatur, Edgewood and Whitehall all meet up with good old Peachtree. Peachtree *Street*, that is. If you are on Peachtree View, or Circle, or Heights, or any of the other seventeen Peachtrees, you've got the wrong Peachtree, my friend, and you are lost, and, in modern Atlanta, chances are you will never be found again.

Near Five Points, which is roughly the center of the downtown area—just a few yards from the original surveyor's stake—you will find, if you know your way, a unique tourist trap called Underground Atlanta. This subterranean relic from Victorian days is actually the one-time commercial center of post-Civil War Atlanta, which vanished beneath a tide of ever-spreading concrete around the turn of the century when viaducts were constructed over the railroad tracks. The streets were raised one level, and this segment of history was mothballed for half of the twentieth century, emerging from its cocoon only recently just in time to accommodate the overflow of visiting Yankees, and to relieve them of their greenbacks. Alcohol flows freely, and in great variety. If you are in a nostalgic mood, Muhlenbrink's Saloon will transport you back to Reconstruction days, complete with mint juleps. Should you want to reconsider the Burning of Atlanta, there's a bar named after that event. As for me, I like Ruby Red's Warehouse, where the banjo-playing is loud and the foot-stomping joyous.

Like I said, Underground Atlanta was reopened for the tourists. So local boys like me hurry down and feed its cash registers because we hate to see the outsiders having more fun than we are.

The night was Friday, the season autumn, the weather warm, and my mood was black. I had just spent another frustrating half hour on the phone with my ex-wife, Lucille, who still lives in what used to be *our* white-pillared antebellum house on Peachtree—View, that is, not Street. The conversation concerned my boy,

Brian, who had just turned eight, and my decision that he ought to spend more time with me than the one afternoon a week the court had allowed. The fact that this limitation was imposed when I was on the road trying to peddle my line of vending machines and had no real time for Brian anyway was no longer valid, I argued. I had my own apartment, my partner Sam Morse did most of the traveling, and I had as much time for the boy as he wanted. But Lucille wasn't interested. In fact, she made it clear that even the one afternoon a week was a little too much so far as she was concerned. I told her that she was only using Brian to punish me, and she told me what a lying, cheating shitheel I was, and we both tried to choke each other through the phone wires, and finally somebody hung up.

Our usual Friday night phone call.

At that time, I still had my own name. I was William Kirby—good old Bill, single again and out to howl on the town.

Well, why not? Was I supposed to spend every night in my apartment drinking beer, watching TV and talking with Gus, my big black Labrador retriever?

I was on my way to hoist a few with Sam Morse, who had just come home from Cedartown with a nice fat order for ten coffee makers and three soft drink machines, and then Sam would go home to his wife and kids, and I would find me a cute little secretary all giggly and not wanting to get involved just yet because there was so much living and loving to taste while you're young, just like old Hugh says in *Playboy*.

Or maybe I would go home to Gus alone, like I most always did.

So, checking that his tie is all snugged up and his jacket collar isn't turned, William Kirby strides up the cobblestoned streets of underground Atlanta, all dim and misty in the gaslights, heading for Ruby Red's Warehouse and the end of his life.

Sam was waiting at the bar, half in the bag already. Sam is a big, husky guy who reminds me of Hoss Cartwright. Quiet, almost timid, devoted to Rita, his sharp-tongued wife who seems always to be right on Sam's heels, like a feisty terrier, chasing him on to bigger and better things. Rita is a beautiful woman, and the three kids haven't spread her hips—or her temper. She is slim as a boy—and her tongue is still sharp as a frog gig. And Sam would have died for her. Except that he didn't get the chance. Instead, he died for me.

As I made my way to the bar, it still wasn't too late. I could have turned around and headed for The Wit's End, where there is usually a nice gaggle of college girls being very intellectual about the imitators of Mort Sahl performing there, and who are ready to expand their horizons—and consciousness—by bringing a little joy into the barren life of an Older Man. I have used that routine so often that you'd think it would be worn out, but just when it begins to pale, a new class arrives and the supply of understanding coeds is renewed. Or I could have given Sam a wave, and we would have wandered over to The Planter's Exchange for some good old cotton state cuisine, all on the expense account, of course. I could have, for Christ's sake, fallen flat on my face and busted my nose or my arm. Anything, except continuing as I did—programmed and locked into an unknown timetable as rigid and unchangeable as the countdown of a missile launch. But the clock was running, and anyway the missile doesn't know it has been programmed, so I joined Sam, and all the rest was as inevitable as sunset and darkness.

Sam was seated next to a tall, long-legged redhead who sipped her martini and tapped her fingers to the beat of the banjo trio, presently murdering "When the Saints Go Marching In." From the studied indifference between them, I could tell that old Sam had tried to score, and hadn't made it. No wonder. Sam trying to swing is ridiculous. No one would ever take him for anything but what he is—a forty-year-old happily married husband and father, out on the town for the one night the wife is away. I felt sorry for him in a friendly, understanding way. I could have gotten him fixed up in ten minutes—but I knew that he would surely find some excuse to back away, so what was the point? Let him enjoy his daydreams of one time latching onto the greatest goddamned head in Atlanta and hauling her off to a motel and boffing the hell out of her nine times straight on a waterbed. Why destroy his harmless fantasy by actually making it possible?

He saw me and held up two fingers. The bartender nodded and bent over his work.

"What are we drinking?" I asked.

"Stingers," said Sam. His voice told me he'd already had at least two.

"Beautiful. Rita will make you sleep out on the porch. Or maybe even under it."

He lifted his half-empty glass. "Not tonight. Here's to Samuel Morse, Liberated Man. Men's Lib, down the hatch."

He swigged. I shuddered. Sam Morse is not your usual down-the-hatch drinker. It can do awful things to him.

"Where is Rita?"

He waved the glass. "She took the kids *and* that gas-guzzling Buick up to Calhoun to visit her mom." He leaned forward, making sure that I understood: *"Rita's* mom, not the Buick's."

The bartender put two deadly looking green stingers before us. The brandy and crème de menthe glistened in multi-colored reflected light from the bandstand.

I hoisted mine. "Congratulations. So you're a weekend bachelor?"

He gave me a sly grin. "Call it a twenty-four-hour pass. Time enough to make out, right?"

"Right."

Sam lowered his voice. "Let's go over to the Playboy Club and see what the bunnies are doing."

"I know what the bunnies are doing," I said. "They're playing bumper pool with the out-of-town salesmen, and that's all they're doing. Who the hell do you know who ever scored with a bunny? Let's just stay here and listen to the banjos."

He nodded, satisfied. He'd made his play. Big Sam, the terror of Atlanta. But if good old Bill didn't want to go along, why Sam could restrain his depravations.

Very drunk-serious, he said, "You know, Bill, it's been a year since you split up with Lucille. Don't you think it's about time you started having some fun? Get out and *live?*"

The long-legged redhead turned to him and said, "Shhh." Sam paid her no attention at all. Now he was straight-arrow Sam, concerned for his partner and buddy. As much as any man could, without being queer, I loved him for it.

"Having fun is what got me in all that trouble, remember?" I tapped his glass. "How many of these bombs have you had?"

Grinning, he said evasively, "The night is young."

"Shhh," repeated the redhead.

He turned to her and sang, "And you're so beautiful." Then, back to me: "Listen, Bill, there's more to life than setting up those damned vending machines and then going home and drinking beer with the black monster you call a dog."

Furious, the redhead said, "Shhhh."

"Same to you, lady," Sam said cheerfully.

I decided this wasn't going anywhere good, so I said, "Let's get moving, Sam, find some action."

He shook his head. "I have just got me an idea," he said. I tried to get a check from the bartender by making writing motions in the air, but it was too late to sidetrack Sam, who had already leaned over and tapped the redhead on the shoulder. Slowly, almost unbelievingly, as if something loathsome and unhuman had appeared in the night and called her by name, she turned.

Smiling, Sam said "Shhhh!"

The redhead said, "I beg your pardon?"

Sam nodded toward me. "You look like a level-headed lady, Red. What would you say to a great guy who splits up with his wife and she takes the kid, and *he* gets custody of the dog?" I waved at the bartender, who was now writing, trying to hurry him up. Relentlessly, Sam went on: "A hot-shot engineer who can make machines *sing*, an all-round good fellow, a genuine hero with a Silver Star he didn't find in a box of Cracker Jack, what would you say to this poor guy who sits around in a rented apartment drinking beer with the goddamned dog? Wouldn't you have a drink with a genuine prince like that?"

I'd gotten the check, and had started to peel off bills to pay it. The redhead nailed me with her eyes, chal-

12

lenging. "Why doesn't the prince ask for himself?" she said.

It was tempting. But somebody had to get Sam home, or the gentle Atlanta gendarmes would slam him into the poky.

"The prince would, lady," I said. "Except at dawn he and his drunken court jester turn into working slobs who have to get down to the warehouse." I hustled Sam to his feet. "Rain check?"

She didn't look away. "Any time," she said.

Sam was mumbling protests as I elbowed him toward the door. Back at the bar, a young soldier wearing a Third Armored patch swaggered up and indicated the seat next to the redhead.

"You mind?" he said.

She withered him with a scornful glance and said, "Are you kidding, sonny?"

THREE

IT IS always a little unnerving, especially when you're on the booze, to come out of a building, look up, and see nothing but cement overhead. The gas street lights poked fuzzy holes in the darkness, but I still had the sensation of being buried alive.

My car was some six blocks away, up in the real world. I prodded Sam.

"Come on, Thimble-Belly. Whatever gave you the idea you could drink stingers?"

Miserably, he said, "Where's your car? I don't feel so good."

"No wonder," I said. "I'm parked over on Alabama Street. Just take it easy."

We turned down a side street, behind the fancy fronts of the night clubs and boutiques. This was garbage can territory and, like back alleys anywhere, had its resident population of surly cats slinking close against the shadowed walls. The music was far behind us now, just an echoing whisper of sound. Our footsteps

14

made hollow taps against the cobblestones. Sam grabbed my arm and hissed, "Shhh!"

Hell, if he hadn't been so sloshed, I probably could have made out with that redhead. Angrily, I said, "Sam, don't start that again."

"I heard something," he said.

"You heard your belly growling," I said. "Come on, let's get you home."

I got him to move another step, then he balked again and held up his hand.

"Listen," he hissed.

I listened and heard voices. So what? We didn't own the alley. Two more drunks arguing. Who the hell cared?

One said, "You're only wasting your time."

The other yelled, "Bastard! You just want more money."

Sam grabbed my arm. Now *he* was in a hurry to be somewhere else.

"Bill, this is trouble," he said. "Let's get out of here."

We should have done just that. But I was curious, and everything else that happened was because of it. I should have taken my cue from the cats, who had played it smart and vanished.

Voice Number One said, "Harry, face it. There just ain't enough money in the world to quiet things down now that the Justice Department's in the act."

The other voice said, "You prick! You're selling me out."

A pause. Then Voice Number One: "Get the hell away from me."

The second man said, "Don't try it, Clem."

Sam Morse tried to drag me back toward the lights and music. "Come *on!*" he urged.

I was ready to go. But then we heard the shot. It was incredibly loud, a booming, alien sound that seemed to echo and roar down the narrow alley like an angry living thing.

Sam turned and ran. I tried to follow, but slipped on an empty beer can and went down to one knee. When I struggled to my feet, I found myself facing a man who had just hurried around the corner.

All I saw at first was his white suit. Very white, very expensive, and very large. He went three hundred pounds, easy. Until a few years ago, he would have been what you call "husky." Now all that had turned to unhealthy fat. Only his eyes were taut, alert. A few years ago, this man could have broken me in half. He used to be tough. Now he probably hired other men to be tough for him. But the pistol was still in his hand. *It* was plenty tough. Tougher than me.

It had been a long time since my hand-to-hand combat days. But what choice did I have? I dropped on one knee, got ready.

White-Suit was puffing for breath, sweating. He started to lift the pistol. I almost jumped him, but didn't when he lowered its muzzle again. He jammed one pudgy fist into a pocket and came out with a horse-choking wad of green bills. He leaned forward and stuffed them down inside my shirt front. I wanted to do something—hit him, run—anything except stand there and submit to those fingers bumping against my chest. But I didn't move.

Rasping, he said, "Be smart, buddy. I don't want trouble. *You* don't want trouble." He backed away from me, toward another alley. "Be smart," he repeated, and then he was gone.

I stared after him. The money itched against my bare skin. I pulled it out and stuck it down in one jacket pocket. Something touched my arm and I whirled, almost striking out.

It was Sam. He jumped back, gasping. "Hey, it's me. Sam. Listen, let's go."

"In a minute," I said, staring at the dark corner from which White-Suit had appeared.

Sam was horrified as I stepped toward it. "Are you *crazy?*" he whispered.

"You can wait here," I told him. "I'll just be a minute."

He stood for a moment, then decided he'd rather be with me than alone, and hurried to catch up.

We turned the corner, and it was exactly as I had expected—the obligatory body sprawled across a nest of garbage cans. He was slim, middle-aged, and clutched a pistol in his right hand. Above his head, on the very pinnacle of a stack of beer cases, a gray cat perched and, as we appeared, it hissed and leaped

17

toward us. For a moment it was as if we were being attacked by some crazed demonlike creature. Sam yelled and backed against a wall, and the cat ran between us.

"That's *it!*" he yelled. "Are you coming?"

"Sam, wait a minute—"

"Like hell I'll wait a minute," he said, and took off.

The dead man drew me toward him compellingly. But then I heard sirens in the distance. We had not been the only ones to notice the shot.

Sam stopped at the corner and looked back. "Bill," he called, "I'm not getting mixed up in any murder. Are you coming or not?"

The sirens were closer.

"Wait for me," I said, and started running too.

FOUR

NO MORE Peachtree View for me. Now I lived on prosaic 14th Street, just a few blocks north of Georgia Tech. When Lucille and I split, Sam had mentioned the apartment building just a block away from his house. I investigated, and when the manager agreed to accept Gus as a tenant, I signed the lease. This area had originally been a quiet, middle-class district, but now the small apartment buildings are springing up like weeds in a tomato patch.

It was still early, and the pale glare of thousands of television picture tubes oozed out into the night from Atlanta windows. In my car, all was quiet. I didn't feel any too proud about the way I'd acted in the alley.

I stopped at the curb in front of Sam's sprawling split-level ranch with two and a half baths.

"You'll thank me tomorrow," he said.

"Sure."

Urgently, he said, "Bill—*it's none of our business!*"

"I heard you," I said. Then, "You want to come over to my place for a drink?"

He hesitated, then said, "I'd better not. I . . . well, I promised Rita I'd call her before the Late Show goes on."

I checked my watch. Ten after eleven.

"Time for a quick one."

"Maybe tomorrow," he said miserably. He wasn't very happy about tonight, either. Getting out of the car, he looked back and said, "See you in the morning?"

"Right," I said. "We shouldn't have to put in more than a couple of hours, just get those machines in shape for shipment Monday."

"See you," he said.

I drove up the block and parked in my very own slip in the lot outside the apartment building. It had my number on it—3–B. I let the engine idle a little, checked the dash. I drive a 1970 Fury. The only thing furious I have noticed about it so far is the way it gobbles up voltage regulators. And the amp meter was registering high charge again. You'd think today's mechanics, at ten bucks an hour, could find wherever the hell the short was so I could allow the voltage regulator industry to sink into a period of recession.

I wondered what was on the Late Show. . . .

Gus met me at the door, as usual. This was slightly more of a production than it sounds. Gus enjoys the good life, and weighs almost as much as I do, and when

I opened the door, he hurled all one hundred and fifty pounds at me, slamming both front paws against my shoulders and slathering my face with doggy kisses.

I mauled his head with both hands, and he made that joyous whimpering sound Labs do so well. "Gus," I growled in my deepest voice, "how the hell have you been?"

He had been lonely, and demonstrated it by shoving his huge head under one of my arms and shaking it back and forth. Gus doesn't fool around. If he likes you, he shows it. Of all the lousy things that came out of nine years of marriage, ending up with custody of Gus was one of the better ones.

He was only two years old when we split. Hell, who needed a dog? I had in mind lots of staying out all night to make up for the unbroken string of unsatisfying bed episodes during the past couple of years. But Lucille soon put me straight.

"He's your dog," she told me. "You can take him with you, or I'll call the pound and have them put him away."

Nice lady.

I loved her, once.

What went wrong? How many times have marriage counselors and divorce judges tried to find the answer to *that* one? So far as my own knowledge goes, not once in all the millions of divorces our courts have presided over, has any jurist ever leaned forward and, in his best Lionel Barrymore voice, announced, "My children, I have discovered what's troubling your marriage."

Trouble troubles us, I guess.

How do you fix trouble?

You run away from it.

That was Sam Morse's answer, as evidenced tonight. And Sam was probably right.

Screw it. I needed a beer. Time for my nightly game with Gus.

"Where the hell are your manners?" I growled. "I'm thirsty." I'm no kook. I don't believe dogs can listen and understand what you say. But they are sensitive to the tone of your voice and to your mood, and there are occasional key words they recognize. "Sit." "Stay." "Heel." And "Thirsty."

Gus padded to the refrigerator, reached up with his paw, and neatly flicked open the door. He had trouble doing it at home with the old one we had with the spring latch. But this apartment was up to date, early Danish-copy and Sears, Roebuck furnishings, which includes a refrigerator with a magnetic catch. Gus learned this trick when he was on a diet and Lucille was hiding his dog food in the frig.

"Jesus, I'm thirsty," I repeated.

Gus reached his huge black head inside, took a can of Rebel Yell beer in his teeth and padded back into the living room with it. I popped the tab and foam flew.

"Many thanks," I said. "But you forgot to shut the door." "Door," was the other key word in the game.

Gus went back into the kitchen and pushed the door shut with his shoulder.

Such excellent service must not go unrewarded. Gus has a bowl which sits on the floor near my TV chair. This is not a food bowl, nor a water bowl. Those are in the kitchen. This is Gus's beer bowl, and as payment for his efforts, I poured him a generous slug. He looked at me, and I gave the final signal of our game.

"Cheers," I said.

He drank. So did I. He burped. I was more polite.

"Slob," I said.

He smiled, if it can be said that a dog smiles. Anyway, he had a friendly look. I know he wasn't sloshed. Gus can handle a couple of quarts with no trouble at all. He put his head on my knee, and I patted it.

"Well, Gus old buddy," I said, "once again we're up the creek without a paddle."

He rolled his eyes up at me. Gus doesn't understand words, as I am willing to admit, but he is a whiz at meaningful voice tones.

I hauled out the wad of money and showed it to him. He wondered if it were something good to eat, and stuck his nose close to find out. I guess he smelled Mr. White-Suit and didn't like the odor, because he drew back with a huffy sniff.

"My reaction exactly," I said, riffling through the bills. They came to $320. "Over three hundred bucks. What the hell am I supposed to do? Give it to the cops?

23

Burn it? Spend it on beer?"

Gus rolled his eyes. Beer is another word he understands. He headed for the refrigerator. I called him back.

"Forget it, old buddy," I said. "Screw them all but six, and save them for pallbearers. We don't need any more trouble than we've got. Who the hell cares about two gorillas shooting it out in Underground Atlanta? What do they have to do with us anyway? Let's mind our own business."

Gus went "Wuff!" which meant somebody was just about to ring my doorbell.

My doorbell rang.

It was Sam Morse. "Hey," I said, letting him in. "I thought you were watching the Late Show. What's up?"

He rushed over to the TV set and turned it on.

"I told you," he gasped, breathless. "You're going to thank me."

The TV set didn't come with the apartment, so it is only a 14-inch black and white Panasonic. Both color sets stayed with Lucille, which is only right, her lawyer keeps telling me.

The picture faded in, and I saw what looked very much like the front of Ruby Red's Warehouse in Underground Atlanta. I looked again, and by God, it *was* the Warehouse. An ambulance was parked across the street, and there were three or four police cars with revolving lights that went BLINK-BLINK-BLINK and people running every which way, and then two guys in white coats came out of an alley, wheeling a cart with a sheet over it and there was something lumped up under the sheet.

An announcer was talking over the picture, and actually we got four or five of his words before the picture appeared, but they didn't make any sense until we saw the cart and its sheeted burden. He was saying, ". . . typical gangland killing. The victim was in Atlanta to testify at a Department of Justice hearing concerning graft and corruption in the meat packing industry."

Then they flashed a newsreel sequence of a great big crowd on the tube, and the announcer said, "Just hours before his murder, union official Clem Hawkins spoke to Channel Nine about corruption in the vital meat packing industry."

I saw a face in close-up and yelped, "Hey, that's the guy that got killed."

"Shhh," said Sam Morse for about the twentieth time that night.

A reporter stuck a microphone in the skinny guy's face and asked, "Mr. Hawkins, why are you here today?"

The skinny guy answered, "It's about time the truth came out."

The reporter asked, "Do you have specific information for the Crime Strike Commission?"

Hawkins answered, "Let's just say, sir, that I'm not here whistling 'Dixie.' "

Sam Morse said, "See, Bill? I told you, you're going to thank me."

Then we saw more newsreel footage of other witnesses gathered outside the federal courthouse.

The announcer said, "One shipping expediter, rumored to be closely associated with the warehouses under investigation, Harry Cade, said—"

We saw a big close-up of Mr. White-Suit himself, and he said, "No comment."

"Oh, my God," I said, choking on my beer.

Sam Morse began, "That's—"

And I finished, "—the *other* guy in the alley!"

FIVE

SAM was dead set against my going to the police. I didn't particularly like the idea myself, but I couldn't just sit there drinking beer, knowing what I did.

The runaround I got from the desk sergeant almost sent me out into the street again, but then somebody higher up took charge and the next thing I knew, Sam and I were in the District Attorney's office. He introduced himself as Fred Boyson. He had a pale, sallow complexion, and reminded me of an undertaker. There was another man in the office, an older man with thin gray hair and a perpetual worried expression on his face. I couldn't put my finger on it, but I got the impression he didn't really approve of Fred Boyson.

He shook my hand. "I'm Harvey Baker, with the Justice Department."

Boyson added, "Mr. Baker's in charge of Atlanta's Strike Force Against Organized Crime."

"That's impressive," I said. Boyson scowled. Baker

smiled. That showed me where their heads were fastened on.

"Of course, this murder investigation is a city matter," said the D.A. "But, as a courtesy, Mr. Baker is here to represent Justice."

"The Justice *Department,*" Baker corrected gently.

Sam Morse was puffing at one of the few cigarettes I'd ever seen him smoke, saying nothing.

Boyson handed me a stack of photographs. "Take your time," he said.

Since there were only five or six, and only one was obviously Harry Cade, it took me a fast three seconds. I handed Cade's picture to Boyson.

"That's him," I said.

He reshuffled the photos and gave them to Sam, who flipped through them and handed the whole pack back to Boyson, who stared at him.

"Mr. Morse?" he prodded.

Sam shrugged. "It was dark," he said. "I never saw any faces."

This seemed to intrigue Baker, who leaned forward. "Then why did you come down here at all?" he asked.

Sam turned to him. "I just wanted you all to know that it was goddamned dark in that alley. Too dark for me to see anybody's face." He jerked his head toward me. "And too dark for Bill to be sure, either."

Boyson started to say something, but the Justice Department man cut him off. "Mr. Morse—Mr. Kirby—

believe me, I know how difficult it is for the ordinary citizen to get himself mixed up in something like this."

"Speak for yourself," said Sam. "I'm not mixed up in anything, and neither is Bill, not if he's got the sense the Lord gave a duck."

"I know how you feel," said Baker. "You're afraid of wasting time, of being wrong. Of retribution. But sooner or later, somebody *has* to come forward, or how can we ever stop the Harry Cades?"

"Buddy," said Sam, "I guess that's just your problem."

Boyson said, "If you'll look at these photos again—" and Baker cut him off.

"You read the papers, Mr. Morse," he said. "You must surely know how effective our Strike Forces have been. We're not just indicting, we're *convicting* the higher-ups. For the first time, they're going to jail in considerable numbers."

"Yeah," said Sam. "And how many of your witnesses are going to the hospital?"

Boyson jumped in. "This is a city matter, remember. Protection is our department. You don't have to worry, Mr. Morse. We'll take care of you."

"Hooray," said my partner. "Just like you took care of that poor slob who fingered Willie Sutton?"

"That happened up North," Boyson said.

"They shot him in the head, remember?" said Sam, looking directly at me.

I liked all this less by the minute.

"What are the odds?" I asked Baker. "I mean, will my testimony really do any good?"

Boyson answered. "We've already got hard evidence against Cade. Your eyewitness identification will slam the door on him."

I hesitated. "Well—"

Baker said, "Don't feel we're pressuring you, Mr. Kirby. I know this is a big decision."

Sam said, "Not for me it isn't."

"Look," I said, getting up, "why don't I let you know? This is something I've got to think over."

Boyson said, "It's your duty—" and Baker waved him down with one hand.

We left.

When we were out of the room, Boyson threw his pencil down on the desk and swore. "Some citizens," he said.

"I don't blame them," said Baker. "Why on earth should they trust us?"

And as we waited for our elevator, a good-looking secretary at one of the outer office desks switched off the intercom she'd been listening to and jotted down two names on a slip of paper.

She slipped the names into her purse.

They were "William Kirby" and "Sam Morse."

* * *

As we drove back to the warehouse, Sam gave me the needle.

"Didn't you get shot at often enough overseas? Now you want to take up playing moving target as a hobby. Beautiful."

"Simmer down, Sam," I said. "I didn't tell them I'd testify."

"You didn't tell them you wouldn't." He lit up another cigarette, his hand shaking. "Bill, this isn't something you fool around with. That guy Cade is in big with the mob, the syndicate, the Mafia, the Brotherhood, whatever the hell it is they call it today."

Stubbornly, I said, "And it's about time they started nailing guys like Cade to the wall."

"So let somebody else do the nailing. What's the point, Bill? You know as well as I do what'll happen. Even if they convict him, he'll draw ten years, and only serve three, and meanwhile, you, Bill Kirby, will become public enemy number one. I'm not making this up. You've read the papers. You know how many guys end up floating in the river."

I knew he was right. I felt silly for even having gone downtown. But once I decide to do something, I hate to give it up. I said, "Damn it, Sam, I don't know *what* the hell to do."

"*I* know," he told me. "Let it drop. Ask yourself, is it worth all the hassle you could get? Just to lock Harry Cade up for a couple of years?"

Slowly, I said, "I guess not."

*   *   *

I got Fred Boyson on the second ring. He was very pleasant at first, until I told him why I was calling.

"Now hold on," he said. "You can't back away now."

"I never told you I'd testify. And I just don't see any point in it."

"I'll subpoena you," he warned. "I've already got your formal identification."

"And you told me you've also got hard evidence against him."

"But I need yours to be certain."

"I'm sorry," I said.

"Is it protection you want? You've got it. Police escort around the clock. You can even check into a hotel suite if you want to. The city'll pay for it."

This made me mad. Was I some kid he could grease? "Shove it," I said. "You know better than that. If they really want to get somebody, they can. You couldn't protect President Kennedy, or Bobby, or Martin Luther King. And those were really important men, you could spend millions trying. Me, I'm not important, not unless I try to make myself important, and I don't think I want to."

He said, "You can't just sit back and let somebody else do all the work. We all have to make sacrifices."

"Is that a fact, Mr. District Attorney? And exactly what sacrifices have you made recently?"

"Oh, hell!" he said. There was a pause. Then, "Look, Kirby, I wouldn't be pushing so hard if I didn't really and truly believe this is our real chance to even up some old scores with Cade and his bunch."

"I'm sorry. They're not *my* old scores. You can subpoena me if you want, but don't depend on what I'll say on the stand."

He waited again before answering. "Look, don't make your decision today. Give it a day or so."

"I'll think it over," I said. "But don't hold your breath."

"Call me on Monday," he said.

"I will," I told him. He hung up.

Then there was another click, just as if somebody had been listening on an extension.

That afternoon, they threatened me.

I'd driven down to the airport to pick up some parts that were being air-freighted from New York. I was sitting in the third-floor bar, killing time waiting for the flight and having a beer when a helicopter landed outside in the big yellow circle painted on the runway.

The man next to me at the bar shook his head. He was slim, dark-haired, with a big cigar poking out of his jaw. He had a slight accent. In view of what came next, this sounds corny, and all the anti-defamation groups will start yelling, but his accent seemed Italian. Or maybe he was from Brooklyn. I can't tell the difference.

"I still don't believe those things can really fly," he said.

Not really paying attention, I said, "Sometimes I doubt it myself."

"You ever go up in one?"

"Overseas."

"You're taking your life in your hands," he said.

"It isn't that bad," I said, looking at him. He was obviously being more than idly polite.

He puffed at his cigar and the smoke nearly choked me. "Yeah," he said. "I guess the odds are with you. But of course, odds *do* change."

There was something wrong with this conversation. I waited for his next move.

It came. He leaned forward and his voice lowered. "As long as a guy sticks to his own business, he's got everything going for him. It's only when he starts shoving in where he shouldn't be that he gets in trouble."

I put my glass down. "What the hell are you getting at, mister?"

"Getting at? I'm just passing the time of day."

"Pass it somewhere else," I said, starting to get up.

He blocked my movement with his outstretched leg. "That's not very friendly," he said.

"Move out of my way," I told him.

"You seem nervous, Mr. Kirby," he said. That sent a chill running down my back. This wasn't just some obnoxious drunk. He knew my name. "Maybe you ought to take a vacation. Maybe your boy, Brian, might like to take in the rides at Disney World."

34

I stiffened. I started to say, "You son of a bitch—" but he kept on talking.

"Forget about showing up in court. That way, you'll find the tickets, and reservations, and even some cash money in your mailbox. That's better than some of the things you *could* find there."

I twisted off the stool and stood up. So did he.

Backing away just enough to be out of easy reach, he said, "Maybe you've been listening to that half-assed D.A. again? Maybe you don't really believe this thing could be very serious for you and your family? That would be a mistake, Mr. Kirby."

I reached for him, and he backed away, and some tables were between us. By the time I got around them, he was out the door, and the bartender was looking at me funny. I stopped, trembling.

"Give me another beer," I said.

SIX

THE woods were all violent green and rich brown. Tall pine trees and heavy oaks with their limbs brushing the ground surrounded me. The oaks dripped Spanish moss, and the scent of magnolia filled the air.

I heard the twig break under a careless foot. I made a dive for the bushes, but I was too late. The pistol was only inches away from my face. I swallowed hard.

"No," I said.

The pistol pressed closer.

"All right," I said. "You've got me. Just don't shoot."

I heard a laugh. It was high, shrill, almost like a woman's. Then the voice: "You lost. So long."

The finger pressed against the trigger. I covered my eyes with one hand.

And the stream of water pumped out and got my hair all wet.

I threw myself down, arms spread wide, and groaned.

This was Sunday. My afternoon with Brian. We were

36

playing jungle scout, and he'd just surprised me, which was fine, but now he shot me a second time with the water pistol, which wasn't.

I sat up. "Enough already. I'm dead."

Brian smiled hesitantly, afraid I was really mad. Uncertainty . . . that's the expression I've seen on his face so often since the divorce. That, and the stammer. Like many boys, he always stammered a little when excited or tired, but it had gotten worse in the past year. I tousled his hair. At eight, he had decided he was too big for embraces.

"I got you again," he said, delighted. "T-That's two for me."

"You've got no respect for your old man," I said.

Realistically, he said, "Oh, I don't know. I think maybe you just *let* me c-c-catch you."

I punched him on the arm, not too hard. He grinned. I liked that better. It was real.

We went over to the edge of the lake and scrunched down on our hunkers, flipping stones into the water. He was all golden in the sun, and his hair was bleaching out. I felt a surge of something good inside my chest as I looked at him. My son.

Then I glanced at my watch, and the grin was gone from his face.

He said, "I guess it's getting late, huh?"

"Six-thirty," I admitted. "We'll have to get moving soon or your mother'll skin me alive."

He studied me. "Are you still m-m-mad at her?"

I shook my head. "No, Brian. I'm not mad at her."

"T-t-t—" He gave up on the word, substituted another. "*Well*, why don't you live with us any more?"

I skipped a rock. It made three bounces. Pretty good. He waited, and I had to answer.

"Well, buddy," I said. "It's pretty complicated."

He put on his version of an adult face and nodded. We had already had our man-to-man talk about this.

"Oh, I know you're d-d-d-divorced," he said. "But why?"

"I did something wrong," I told him. "I didn't think it was terribly wrong at the time, but your mother did."

Persistently, he said, "But if you're not m-m-m—if you're not *angry* with her, and she's not m-*mad* at you, why don't you come back and live with us?"

I stared at the water. Slowly, I said, "Brian, to tell the truth, I just don't know."

I heard him give a gasp, as if he had hurt himself. I looked up, just in time to see his eyes widen as he cried, "Daddy!"

"What's wrong?"

He pointed. "By your foot. There's a snake!"

I froze, turned my head slowly.

Coiled near my leg was a gray, mottled bull snake, half asleep in the sun. He had been lying in the grass all this time, afraid to move. Hoping we would go away without hurting him.

"Take it easy, son," I said. "Don't scare him."

"*I'm* the one who's s-s-scared," Brian said, trying to laugh.

"You shouldn't be," I said. "He's harmless." I reached for the snake. He tightened his coil and hissed.

"He sounds mad," Brian said, looking closely. "How do you know he isn't poison?"

I pointed at the bull's head—rounded, almost an extension of the neck. "See how round the back of his head is? The poisonous ones have heads shaped like an arrowhead." I moved my hand toward him, palm flattened down toward the flicking tongue. "Easy . . . easy . . . nobody's going to hurt you."

Mr. Bull Snake had all he could take. He struck at me, but his nose bounced harmlessly off my outstretched palm. I'd learned that trick in the jungles of Southeast Asia, where entertainment was at a premium. My platoon sergeant used to draw a crowd by just playing his harmonica.

"Watch out!" Brian yelled.

I slipped my hands under the snake. You mustn't pick one up by the neck, or you will hurt it. Give him lots of support. I held him just behind the head with one hand, and let the other rest under his belly.

"He's just an old bull snake, Brian," I said. "He's friendly enough if you don't scare him. Here—" I held the snake out to him. Hesitantly, he took it.

"Hey!" he said, surprised. "He's not slimy."

"Remember what I told you. Nothing in the woods

39

.will hurt you unless you hurt or frighten it first."

He stroked the bull snake's shell-like nose. "Can I keep him?"

I got up. "My God, no. Your mother would shoot me. Come on, sport, let him go. It's time we got on the road."

Brian released the snake, and it glided out into the water and swam away. He stared after it, then looked up at me, and the good grin was back.

"You know what, Daddy? I wasn't scared at all."

We got back to the car, and the traffic was bad, so I took all the back roads and short cuts I knew, staying away from the interstates where cars were backed up bumper to bumper. I made good time, and it was only a few minutes after eight when I pulled into the driveway, but Lucille was already waiting on the porch, that tight, pained expression of anger she wears so well nailed down tight on her otherwise lovely face.

The house on Peachtree View was one of the nicer ones in the area, and it should have been, for the dough it cost—and continues to cost—me. It is fake antebellum, but only an expert could tell the difference. To the average person, driving up its circular roadway was just like arriving at Tara. You expect Scarlett O'Hara to come out. Instead, Brian and I got his mother, with her mad face. Behind it, she is a small tawny blonde, and I could still see vestigial traces of the lusty, happy girl I'd married one crazy night in Key West.

Brian jumped out of the car and rushed up to her and she gave him a protective hug.

Over his shoulder, she said, "You're late."

"I'm sorry," I said. "We hit traffic."

That was better than admitting I'd deliberately overstayed my allotted time. Then Brian blew it.

"We caught a s-s-snake, Mom. Daddy let me hold him and—"

Repulsed, she said, "That's nice. You'd better wash your hands."

He started to rush into the house. She stopped him.

"Say good night to your father."

He came back and, shyly, held out his hand. I took it.

"Good night, Daddy."

"Good night, son."

"What are we going to do next Sunday?"

Awkwardly, aware of Lucille, I said, "We'll think of something."

"Maybe we can go to S-s-s—" He gave up on the word "Six" and substituted "*All* those Flags over Georgia."

This is a big amusement park copied from Disneyland, ten miles west of Atlanta.

"Maybe," I said. "You be good, y'hear?"

He ran into the house. There was a strained pause.

Lucille broke it. "I don't suppose you want a drink or anything?"

"No, thanks."

I turned to go, but I didn't make it.

In a rush, she said, "I would think you would remember about the Sunday traffic and not worry me sick—"

"I'm sorry," I said. "I lost track of the time."

She stared at me, and her lip quivered. I wondered what was going through her mind. We had shared the same house and bed for nine years, and now I realized I didn't know one damned thing about her. From the very second she found out about me and the girl who had been my secretary, Lucille had changed into another person, a stranger with whom I could no longer communicate.

"Do you need anything?" I asked. "I mailed the mortgage check yesterday, and . . ."

"No," she said. "We're fine. We've always been fine, that way."

It was on the tip of my tongue to tell her we'd been fine in every other way, too, that what I'd done was nothing unique nor was it unforgivable, but we had eaten that corn bread already and there wasn't any point in starting over.

"Say good-bye to Brian for me," I said. "I'll pick him up next Sunday, same as usual."

As I drove away, I saw her staring after me.

The apartment was very quiet when I got home. I used the key, opened the door, flicked on the light, and something was very *wrong*.

"Gus—?" I called.

He didn't come.

I shut the door and moved into the living room.

42

Everything seemed in order.

But where the hell was Gus? Could he have jumped out the window?

I started for the bedroom, stopped.

Now I heard it.

A steady drip-drip-drip, as if a faucet were leaking in the kitchen.

I didn't want to, but I opened the door. It was heavy and hard to move.

Then I saw what was hanging on the door.

It was Gus.

His throat had been cut, and then they had pinned him to the door with a long butcher knife.

It was his blood that I'd heard dripping into a glistening pool on the floor.

"Oh, my God, no!" I gagged, backing away. But the relentless dripping sound followed me. I forced myself back into the kitchen, hoisted Gus's limp body with one arm and pulled out the knife with my other hand. It had been thrust through a square of paper that was now blood-matted.

I read:

> This is what happens to barking
> dogs and their pups, too.

Lowering Gus to the gory floor, I closed the door on him. When I picked up the phone, I saw my fingers were smearing blood over it. I dialed, and the District

Attorney's office answered. That was lucky. I hadn't really hoped to find anyone there on Sunday night.

"Let me speak to Mr. Boyson."

"This is Boyson," he said.

I told him who I was and went on, "You remember what you said to me about Harry Cade?"

"What?"

"That you wanted to nail him to the wall?"

"I guess I did use those words."

"Use them again, Mr. Boyson. Because that's what I want to help you do. Nail that no-good bastard to the wall."

There was a pause. Then he asked, "Has something happened?"

"Let's say I had a chance to do some thinking. What do you want me to do next?"

"Can you come down here in the morning to sign a statement?"

"I'll be there. But you've got to protect my ex-wife and my boy."

"I'll send a car right out," he said. "What's the address?"

I gave it to him, and he thanked me, and we hung up.

Slowly, I turned toward the kitchen.

SEVEN

THEY say the wheels of justice grind exceedingly fine. I don't know about that, but I can tell you from personal experience that they grind exceedingly slow. Somehow I thought they'd whip Cade into jail and we'd have the trial the next day and it would be all over.

It didn't work out that way. Weeks went by. Sam Morse was pissed off at me, and Lucille dodged my phone calls. Sunday, when I went out to pick up Brian, nobody was home.

The next day, I caught up with her at the supermarket. There was a policeman outside the house, and when I showed him my I.D., he told me where she was.

"I thought you were supposed to be watching her," I said.

"I'm watching the house," he said. "That's all they told me to do."

"Great," I said, and drove off.

She was down at the end of the store, in the meat department, and she wasn't any too happy to see me.

"What do you want?" she said.

"I want to talk to you."

"What about? That policeman in my front yard?"

"He's just there to protect you."

"Well, if his assignment is to protect me against my neighbors, he's doing a good job. Everybody's scared to come over. Thank you very much for getting me into another one of your messes."

"I'm sorry, Lucy," I said, trying to help push her cart. She shoved my hand away. "I didn't know it would be like this."

"Oh?" she asked. "And exactly what did you think it would be like, with your name splashed over every newspaper front page in town?" She stopped moving and stared at me. "Damn it, Bill, the thing I can't forgive is that you didn't even *talk* to me about it. You just went ahead and did it, exactly like that other—mess. That wasn't necessary, either. If you'd only told me you were unhappy, given me some hint—"

"Let's not rake that up again," I said. "I made a mistake, and God knows I'm paying for it."

"Well," she said, almost whispering, "I think you've just made *another* mistake, and who's paying for this one? Brian and me! We're the ones who may get hurt. Haven't you caused enough trouble? Did you have to do this to us, too?"

I just couldn't seem to get through to her, but I tried again. "Honey, I couldn't help it. I mean, I *did* see him, that man Cade, and—"

46

She cut me off. "So what? You saw him, so what?"

"Look, I didn't *want* to get involved—"

"Oh, *no!*" She spat the words close into my face. "You couldn't *wait!*"

"If they hadn't started pushing me around—"

"You never gave *us* a thought—"

"Then they killed Gus—"

Neither of us was hearing a word the other said. But the other shoppers were. We were giving them quite a show.

"So you set out to get *even!*" she accused.

"Lucy, people are looking."

"Fine, let them look. Let them get a *good* look at the great big hero." She stopped suddenly, choking on the last words. The storm was over. And the gulf between us was wider than ever.

In a new tone, she asked, "All right, why are you here? What do you want?"

"I came over yesterday. You weren't home."

"I took Brian to the zoo."

"I'm supposed to see him on Sundays."

"And you're supposed to *care* about him," she said, her voice breaking. "You're supposed to protect him—"

Things were getting out of hand again. "I *do* care about him," I said. "But—"

"Oh, go!" she shrilled. "Go, go! Win your medals over someone else's body—"

I touched her shoulder. "Please, Lucy."

She softened. "Damn it, Bill, it's not *fair.*"

"I know it isn't," I admitted. "I'm sorry. Go ahead, be mad at me. But don't take it out on Brian."

"I didn't mean to," she said.

"Things will be all right, Lucy."

She nodded. "All right. The same time?"

"Same time. Thanks." I gave her a peck of a kiss on the cheek. She didn't draw away, but she didn't respond either. "You tell him we'll even take a ride on the log flume."

"I will," she said. Then, as I turned to go, "Bill—be careful."

When I got out to the warehouse, late, Sam was waiting outside. I saw a police car driving off.

I parked, and he came over. "What's up?" I said.

"Come on inside," he said angrily. "You'll see what's up."

"Why were the cops here?"

"Ask your friend, the D.A." And that was all he would say until I'd gotten out of the car and followed him into the warehouse.

It was a mess.

Someone had been very busy with a sledgehammer. The ten coffee makers that were supposed to go out to Cedartown would be going to the junk heap instead. Their innards were strewn all over the floor, and covered with thick motor oil.

"It was like this when I came in this morning," Sam

said. "Now, who do you suppose would do a thing like this to two law-abiding citizens like you and me?"

Sickened, I said, "They know you're not involved, Sam. I'm the only one listed as a witness."

"And I'm your partner. Would you like to hear about the phone calls we've been getting, partner? About the guy who calls Rita every morning just after I leave the house, and tells her to go down to the bus station and open a certain locker, where she'll find my head in a bowling bag? My kids walk home from school. Would you like to meet the other guy, the one who says he's going to wait until they're crossing Tenth Street, and then he's going to nail them with his two-ton truck? He says the only reason he hasn't done it before now is that they've been too spread out, and he's trying for a triple, because that means extra points."

His voice was ragged. I changed the subject. "What else did they get here, Sam?"

He laughed, right on the edge of hysteria. "Everything, buddy boy. Come on, take a look."

We picked our way through the wreckage. They'd been thorough, and at least one of them knew something about vending machines. Even those that hadn't been too smashed up had the vital parts destroyed. I estimated the loss at eighty percent or more. And not covered by insurance, I thought bitterly. Coin-operated machines are too vulnerable, in their lonely outposts of the night. I remembered, when I was a kid, newspaper vendors would leave a stack of papers on a corner with a little bowl for people to put their money in. Try that today.

Bitterly, Sam said, "They've got a sense of humor, too, your buddies. Look what I found on the door this morning."

He showed me the sign. It read:

SORRY, CLOSED FOR REPAIRS

I tore it to pieces and threw it in the garbage can.

"Bill," said Sam Morse, "are you still going to testify?"

"I've got to," I said.

Sourly, he said, "I wish we hadn't gotten mixed up in this thing."

"So do I," I said.

When I reported the warehouse vandalism to the D.A., he swore.

"I'm sorry, Bill. I didn't think they'd go this far."

"Well, you thought wrong."

"I'll double the protection. As soon as I hang up." He hesitated. "Is that all right?"

"Don't worry," I said. "I'm not pulling out. I'll be there. You'll win your goddamned case."

"I'll get men around the clock," he said.

I told him, "Just get it over with, that's what you can do."

*　　*　　*

50

And, finally, the trial did begin. But it dragged on and on; even selecting a jury took two days. It was Friday morning before I was taken down to the courthouse.

It was mobbed. As Boyson got out of the car, the reporters pressed in around him like a swarm of defensive football players swallowing the quarterback. I heard the barrage of their questions.

"Where's your witness, Mr. District Attorney?"

"Do you expect a conviction?"

"Are you sure your witness will be here?"

Nodding at me to slip out the other door of the car, Boyson said, "He'll be here."

One reporter said, "This wouldn't be the first time a witness against Harry Cade changed his mind and didn't show up."

Then the reporters spotted me, and they were on my heels in full cry like a pack of coon dogs hot on the scent.

"Hey, Mr. Kirby, can you give us a statement?"

"Sorry," I said. "I'm saving it for the jury."

"The odds were nine to five you wouldn't show," another told me. "Do you have any comment on that?"

"Only that it's too bad I couldn't get a piece of the action."

They followed us right up to the door. One called, "Aren't you scared?"

"Sure I'm scared," I told him. "Wouldn't you be?"

The guards stopped them there. As we walked down

the hall, Boyson said, "It's too bad your partner wouldn't testify, too. We'd have a much better case."

"Lay off Sam," I said. "You've got me. That's enough."

"Having second thoughts?"

"Sure," I said. "Second thoughts on top of second thoughts. My knees are knocking, if you want to know. If you expected John Wayne, you picked the wrong boy."

I sat around most of the day, listening to a parade of witnesses from the prosecution, tying Cade in with corruption in the meat packing industry. Most of their evidence got thrown out by the judge as not bearing on the case, over the bitter protests of Fred Boyson. Cade's attorney was a sharp cookie named Harper, and he nailed every inconsistency, every weakness of testimony. I wasn't looking forward to facing him.

Things came to a head around three P.M., when a uniformed policeman took the stand and, with an authoritative air of "Well, now down to business," Boyson produced a surprise piece of evidence.

"And what did you find in the victim's hand?" he asked the policeman.

"A torn bit of cloth."

"Entered as Prosecution Exhibit 'C,'" said Boyson, giving the scrap to the clerk.

"So entered," said the judge. When it had been marked, Boyson took it back and handed it up to the policeman.

"Is this the cloth in question?"

The policeman nodded. "Yes," he said.

"What else do you know about this bit of cloth?"

Reciting words that he did not even seem to understand, the policeman said, "Subsequent investigation proved it was torn from a jacket owned by the defendant, Harry Cade."

Cade leaned over and whispered to one of his henchmen. "How the hell did they get that jacket?"

"I don't know, Harry. I swear to God."

Cade swore, and not to God.

Then it was my turn. I had a little trouble getting my name out, and had to repeat it for the court stenographer. Boyson led me through a recital of my background, my business, my presence that night in Underground Atlanta. He got me all the way to the alley, then asked the clincher:

"Then, in your own words, what happened, Mr. Kirby?"

"A man ran around the corner. He had a pistol. I thought he was going to use it. But then he took out a handful of money instead, and shoved it down my shirt front. 'Be smart,' he told me. 'You don't want trouble.' "

"Did you recognize that man?" Boyson asked.

"Not just then. But later, I saw his picture on TV. And I picked him out of a file of photographs."

"Can you identify him in person?"

"Yes." I pointed. "The defendant, Harry Cade."

Until that moment, Cade had been sitting back,

53

grinning. He didn't look like a man on trial for murder. But now, just for a moment, he lost control. He jumped up before his lawyer could stop him and gave me the old "Fungo!" gesture, with one fist in the air and the other hand clasped around the bicep.

"Liar!" he yelled. "You'll get yours, you fink bastard!"

His lawyer and his friends wrestled him back into his chair. He was still yelling, but I couldn't hear it over the hammering of the judge's gavel and the general commotion in the courtroom.

When order was restored, Boyson asked me, "You're sure of your identification, Mr. Kirby?"

"Positive."

He looked around, walked over and stared down at Cade before asking his next question: "Mr. Kirby, have there been any attempts to prevent you from testifying here this afternoon?"

"Several," I said.

"Tell us about them."

Cade's lawyer objected, and the judge overruled him. I told about the man in the airport bar. And about finding the warehouse wrecked.

"Are you sure that couldn't have been some kind of misunderstanding?" Boyson asked. "Not related to this case?"

"Some misunderstanding," I said, and—in a quiet, low voice—told them about Gus. When I finished, one of the women jurors was crying, and Cade's lawyer looked very unhappy.

He jumped up. "Your honor, there is no evidence—"

"If you mean," I yelled back, "did Gus leave tooth marks on somebody, hell no, that poor dog wouldn't bite anything more lively than a pork chop—"

And Cade's lawyer kept right on with "—linking my client with any of these occurrences—"

So the judge put a halt to it all by bashing his gavel down and sustaining Harper's objection.

Boyson decided to quit while he was ahead, and told Cade's lawyer, "Your witness, Mr. Harper."

Here it came. Harper strolled up and positioned himself directly in front of me. "Thank you," he said. "Now, just one or two points, Mr.—ah—" He consulted a slip of paper, as if my name hadn't been mentioned a dozen times. "Kirby. Is that your real name?"

"It is."

"You've never been known as Siegel? Max Siegel?"

I stared at him. What the hell was this? Over his shoulder, I saw Boyson give a little "Don't worry" wave. I answered, "Kirby's the only name I've ever used."

"Well, we'll leave that for the moment," he said. "Now, Mr. ah—Kirby—just how long have you been in the slot machine business?"

Boyson jumped up. "Your honor!" he protested.

Before the judge could answer, Harper shrugged and said, "Forgive me. Shall we say, *coin* machines."

I had been right. I didn't like this turkey. "You've got a sneaky mouth, buddy," I told him. "We sell soft drinks, coffee, sandwiches, novelties. They're called *vending* machines, and there's at least half a dozen of them out there right now in this courthouse hallway."

He turned to the judge. "Your honor, will you instruct the witness to be responsive?"

The judge smiled down at me. "Mr. Kirby, if you'll answer the question?"

"I've forgotten it," I said.

The judge nodded at the court stenographer, who read back, "How long have you been in the slot machine business?"

Harper made a little gesture. "Make that *vending* machine business. Does that satisfy your terminology, Mr. Kirby?"

"Four years," I said. "Ever since I got out of the Marines."

His eyebrows rose. "Marines? Ah, very commendable. I presume you served in Vietnam."

"Two tours."

His voice went harsh. "Napalming civilians, bombing innocent—"

"Mr. Harper!" This time it was the judge. "That is quite enough."

Harper passed a hand over his forehead. "I'm sorry, your honor. My own feelings about that disgraceful war—"

"Mr. Harper!" Now the judge was mad.

Harper changed the subject. "You say you were, shall we put it, out on the town on the evening in question?"

"Having a few drinks, yeah."

"A few?"

"That's what I said."

"Isn't it a fact that you had so many that you were forcibly ejected from one establishment and barred from entering a second?"

"Hell, no—" I began, and then Boyson leaped up.

"Your honor," he said, "I'm sure it cannot fail to impress the court that my opponent is deliberately trying to blacken Mr. Kirby's reputation by unsubstantiated, untrue allegations which he inserts into the record—and the jury's memory—and then walks away from when challenged to prove them. That business about the alias, the obvious slur on Mr. Kirby's brave war record, the deliberate confusion between legal vending machines and illegal slot machines. I must protest."

"I wondered when you would," said the judge. "And your point is well taken. The counsel for the defense will do well to modify his zeal."

Harper spread his hands. "Forgive me, your honor," he said. "I may have been misled by information which came to me from confidential sources." He turned back to me. "Am I to understand it that you were alone when you witnessed the fatal shooting?"

I hesitated. "I didn't actually witness it. I heard it."

"Ah? And is that how you base your identification of my client? On what you heard?"

"I base it on the fact that he ran around the corner with a pistol in his hand."

"Which only *you* saw."

I caught a glimpse of Sam Morse's face, far back in the courtroom. "I was alone, if that's what you mean."

"That is exactly what I mean," he said. "Now, am I to understand that after you stumbled onto what you considered to be a murder, you accepted payment from the killer and went home and forgot all about it? Why didn't you remain at the scene until the police arrived?"

"I didn't want to get involved."

His eyebrows arched, more at the jury than at me. "But now you *are* involved. How is that, Mr. Kirby?"

What was I supposed to do? Tell them I got mad because they wouldn't stop leaning on me? That I wanted revenge for Gus?

Wasn't that what Lucille had said?

Mumbling, I answered, "I guess I just thought it over."

"Think carefully," Harper said, "A man's life depends on your answer. Isn't there anyone who can substantiate your story of what happened in that alley?"

"I told you I was alone."

He gave a heavy sigh. "Yes, Mr. Kirby, you've told us quite a lot. I think more than enough." He turned to the judge and, with exaggerated distaste, said, "I think I've had all I can take of this witness, your honor."

Boyson started to get up to object, but by then Harper had walked back to his own table. Instead, he said, "Your honor, the prosecution rests."

The judge looked at his watch. "Does the defense intend to call witnesses?"

"We do," said Harper.

"In that case, since it's near the hour for adjournment," the judge said, "this trial will be resumed at ten A.M. Monday. If both attorneys can curb their instincts for the dramatic, perhaps we can give the case to the jury at that time?"

"Our defense will be brief and to the point," said Harper.

Boyson just looked disgusted and said nothing.

Court adjourned. As the room was emptying, Boyson took me aside.

"Why did you lie about Sam Morse?"

"I didn't lie. He wasn't there when I saw Cade. He'd run down the alley."

"You stretched it. I don't think Harper hurt us, but I didn't like the way he kept harping on the possibility of another witness."

Alarmed, I said, "Is there a chance Cade could get off?"

"I don't see how. Bill, if you're nervous, maybe you ought to hole up with us somewhere over the weekend."

"Not a chance. I've promised to take my boy to Six Flags."

"Couldn't you do that after the verdict?"

"It closes for the winter next week. Why, are you afraid Cade's boys will shoot a hole in me?"

Grimly, he said, "Not with the two men I've got guarding you. They're good. But watch yourself."

"Don't worry," I told him. "I can do without *you* any day of the week, but I can't do without *me.*"

I met Sam and Rita in the hall. Sam looked embarrassed. "I didn't know you were going to tell them you were alone," he said.

"Don't worry about it," I said. "No sense in both of us being involved."

He started to say something else, switched in mid-word, and said, "You got to come over for dinner when all this is over. Right, Rita?"

She stared at me, hostility showing in her eyes. *"If* it's ever over."

Shocked, Sam said, "Rita!"

"I'm sorry," she said. "But it happens to be true."

EIGHT

I PICKED Brian up around noon on Sunday. The weekend had been quiet so far. No threatening phone calls, no mysterious encounters. I never saw Boyson's bodyguards, so they were probably as good as he claimed. Either that, or they weren't even there.

Lucille was uneasy about the trial not being over.

"I thought you said it would be finished by now," she said.

"It's nearly done," I said. "My part's over."

"Will he go to jail?"

I tried to grin. "He'd better, after all the trouble we went to."

"Don't joke about it!" she flared. "You've read about what those hoodlums do when they're crossed."

"Lucy," I said, "this isn't any big deal, and neither am I. The law's been after Harry Cade for a long time. This just happens to be the time he got caught."

"Yes," she said, "but you're the one who caught him."

"Not just me," I said. I told her about the piece of torn

jacket. "They'd have nailed him, with or without me."

Brian came out, all slicked up, and we stopped talking about it. As we drove off, I saw her staring out the window at us.

We turned off I–20 at the Six Flags exit, and since it was still early, I was able to park near the gate of the amusement park. Admittance cost $5.75 for me and $4.75 for Brian, but since this covered all the rides and shows, it's a bargain. I hate being nickel-and-dimed to death. I guess it was Walt Disney who started this kind of amusement park, and now they're springing up all over the country under various names. Their secret is that grown-ups get just as big a charge out of the rides and attractions as our kids, whom we take to justify going ourselves.

We got right in line for the log flume ride, because I'd promised Brian. It had just enough of the whiff of controlled danger to make the girls shriek, and I noticed my own knuckles were white against the handrail.

"That was f-f-fun," said Brian. "Can we ride it again?"

"Later," I told him. I wanted to sit down somewhere. That turned out to be in one of the Astro-lift sky rides over the 200-acre park.

And so it went. Two kids at Six Flags—one aged eight, one thirty-four.

You don't know what tired is until you've spent six hours doggedly trying to use every ticket in your admittance book. I finally gave up, with two shows unseen.

"Just one more," Brian pleaded.

I was firm. And exhausted. "Son," I said, "I've had it. Let's go home."

We were parked in Section B–7. Someone must have watched me park the car, because they were waiting.

As we stepped into the main traffic lane, a car shot around the corner and sped down at us, its headlights unlit. Someone yelled, and I gave Brian a shove that sent him sprawling under a parked Chevy. Then I dove myself, and felt the car go by just inches away. It kept going.

People ran over and helped me up. Brian was crying. I grabbed him and checked for obvious injuries. There weren't any, but his clothes were torn and his face was dirty.

"That driver must have been drunk or crazy," a man said, handing me one of my shoes that had come off in the spasm of my dive for safety.

Brian had stopped crying, but replaced it with a nervous hiccough that kept up all the way home.

The porch light was on, and Lucille was watching us as we got out of the car. She threw the door open and started to run toward us. This started Brian crying again and he ran to her, sobbing. She hugged him, staring down at his torn clothing.

"Lucy," I said, "we had a little accident. I—"

That was as far as I got. She slapped my face as hard

as she could. It stung, and I saw bright flashes. She grabbed Brian, dragged him inside, and slammed the door.

I got back in the car and drove home. Along the way, I broke a few speed limits.

Nobody answered this time at Boyson's office. I called the police, and worked my way up to a lieutenant. I told him who I was, and what had happened, and asked for Boyson's home number.

"Well, sir," he said, "that's unlisted."

"I know it's unlisted. That's why I didn't get it from the phone book myself. Why the hell do you think I'm asking you?"

"I'm sorry, sir. What I meant is, we don't have it here either."

"Well, how do you get in touch with him in an emergency?"

"We reach him through his office."

"Nobody's *answering* at his office."

"Could be the duty man went out on a case."

"Well, damn it, *this* is a case. Can't you contact somebody on the radio?"

"Not except in a genuine emergency."

"I told you, this *is* an emergency."

"You were almost hit by a car. That could have been an accident."

"It wasn't, I tell you. Can you prove it was an accident?"

"Can you prove it wasn't, sir?"

"Oh, hell," I said. "Forget it."

I hung up and looked up the number for the Atlanta office of the U.S. Department of Justice.

They answered on the second ring. "Justice Department."

"Hello," I said. "Can I speak with Harvey Baker—"

Then I stopped, because the other voice was still talking. ". . . this is a recording. At the tone, state your name, phone number, and your message. You have thirty seconds."

Beep.

I slammed down the receiver.

"Christ, I'm *thirsty,*" I said.

Gus didn't respond. I'd forgotten.

I got up and went for my own beer.

I never did catch up with Fred Boyson, but I nailed him at the courthouse just before the trial began.

"Where the hell have you been?" I said. "I tried to get you yesterday but nobody could put me in touch."

"Didn't you try my home number?"

"God damn it, it's unlisted."

"But it's on the card I gave you."

His card was in my wallet. And I'd never looked. No point in looking now. He was obviously sure of what he said.

"And," he went on, "it wasn't too smart of you, giving my men the slip."

"Giving *who* the slip? I never saw your men."

"They followed you to Six Flags. They say you ducked out the back exit of one of the shows."

"What the hell, we were taking a short cut. Some shadows you've got there. Did you hear my boy and I were nearly run over?"

"The police had a report on my desk this morning about a call you made reporting an accident."

"Some accident. It was deliberate. Boyson, I don't think much of your protection. It's never around when you need it."

"I'll lean on them. But try to be more cooperative."

I had a fast answer for that, but court was called, and we went in and found soon that Cade's attorney had a big fat surprise for us.

He said, "The Defense calls Mr. Samuel Morse."

Sam got on the stand, and was sworn, and Harper asked him if he was with me that night.

"Yes sir. I'd made a good sale over in Cedartown, and we were celebrating at Ruby Red's Warehouse."

"How much celebrating, would you say?"

Sam tried to grin, but couldn't quite make it. "I lost count of mine," he said. "I don't know how many Bill had."

"Then you started for Mr. Kirby's car?"

"That's right. We took a short cut through the alley."

"What did you see there?"

"Nothing," said Sam.

"Nothing?"

"It was too dark," Sam said. "We heard a shot, and

66

somebody ran out. But I couldn't see his face. Bill Kirby couldn't have either. Like I said, it was too dark."

"Mr. Morse, did you hear your partner's testimony here Friday?"

"Yes sir."

"You heard him identify my client, Harry Cade, as the man he saw in the alley?"

Sam nodded.

"Please state your answer," said the judge, "so the court stenographer can record it."

"Yeah," said Sam. "I heard him."

"Well," said Harper, "how do you explain it, when you yourself are sure it was too dark to see faces?"

"Listen," said Sam. "Bill wouldn't lie, not for anybody. He told you what he thought he remembered."

"Please answer the question. How could he have selected, of all people, Mr. Harry Cade?"

"Well," said Sam, "that night, we saw a news show on TV. And right after they showed the guy who got killed —and we did get a good look at him—they put on some stuff with Mr. Cade. That was the first time I ever saw the man, and I'd swear that's true for Bill, too. He just hooked up the two faces, I guess, and then when he saw Mr. Cade's photo down at police headquarters, he remembered seeing him somewhere. Only he saw him on TV, not in the alley."

"He's lying," I whispered to Boyson. "He recognized Cade on TV, too."

"Shhh," Boyson said.

67

"Your witness, Mr. Boyson," said Harper.

"No questions," said Boyson.

As Sam got down from the stand and hurried to the back of the courtroom, I asked, "Why the hell didn't you question him?"

"Why? To have him tell the jury that he told *us* it was too dark in that alley to see faces? He did, that first day, remember? No, Kirby, your buddy has done us enough harm."

I looked around to find Sam. I couldn't locate him. No wonder he'd been so nervous Friday.

Boyson made a fiery closing argument, hammering home again and again the tangible evidence of the torn bit of jacket. Harper's address, on the other hand, was quiet, underplayed. He simply pointed out that the jury must be very, very sure before sending a man to prison for life.

I guess they weren't so sure. Because they didn't.

When they filed back into the courtroom and the judge asked: "Has the jury reached a verdict?"

"We have, your honor," said the foreman.

The judge nodded, and the clerk went over and collected an envelope. The judge opened it and read, "This jury finds the defendant, Harry Cade, guilty of murder in the second degree. So say you all?"

"Yes sir," said the foreman.

I saw Cade, furious, grab the arm of one of his men and whisper in his ear. There was a lot of noise in the courtroom. The judge banged with his gavel.

"My thanks to the jury for their verdict," he said. "And in particular, my thanks to Mr. William Kirby for having the courage and the sense of duty to come forward and testify in this case, an experience that could not have been pleasant."

This almost sent Cade up the wall. He glared at me.

"Will the defendant stand?" said the judge.

Slowly, Cade got up.

"It is the decision of this court that you shall be remanded to the Federal Penitentiary for a term of not less than four, and not more than twenty years. Case dismissed."

I heard Harper say to Cade, "Don't worry, Harry. We'll appeal."

"Don't waste your breath," Cade said, still staring at me.

Boyson shook my hand. "We couldn't have done it without you, Bill. Thanks."

"Well, don't come back for seconds," I told him. "I don't think I could hack it."

"Juries!" he said angrily. "They *knew* Cade was guilty; the jacket proved that. You were icing on the cake. Then your goddamned partner cast just enough doubt on your story to give them a moment's pause."

"What's this second degree crap?" I asked. "If Cade *was* there, he murdered that guy. If he wasn't, he's innocent."

"It's hard to explain. The jury knew he was guilty, but they didn't think we were completely on the up and up either. So they compromised and brought in Murder Two."

"Well, that's something," I said. "Twenty years is a long time."

"Except it'll be more like three," he said. I remembered, weeks ago, somebody else saying the same thing. Sam Morse. Boyson got up. "Let me buy you a drink."

"Some other time," I told him. "I'm going home to throw up."

I passed Sam and Rita in the back. I didn't go over to speak with them. I didn't know what to say. They made no move toward me either.

In the hall, the man I'd seen sitting near Harry Cade came up to me.

"Kirby," he said, "Harry sent you a message."

"Who the hell are you?" I asked.

"You're a dead man, Kirby," he said. "You may still be walking around, but you're dead."

I stared at him. This was too much. I felt like somebody in an Alfred Hitchcock movie.

Finally, I thought of something to say. "Go haunt a house," I told him.

He moved off into the crowd. I stared after him. Boyson came over.

"What's wrong?" he asked.

"Did you hear that creep?"

"Who?"

"One of Cade's men. He was threatening me."

"With what?"

"Nothing good," I said wearily. "Listen, do things like that really go on? I mean, the trial's over. What's the point in hurting me now?"

"Forget it, Bill," Boyson said.

"I thought you said it was all over once the trial finished."

"It is. Those punks are all mouth. Long on threats, short on action. They won't bother you again. There's nothing in it for them now."

"I hope you're right," I said.

"I am," he promised, "but to be safe, I'll have our guys keep an eye on you for a few days."

"What a mess," I said as we walked toward the street. "Was it worth it? All this hassle, just to lock Cade up for a couple of years?"

"It was worth it," he said. "Cade's only the tip of the iceberg. He won't come out of this clean. He'll lose part of his power. Maybe all of it. Now that we know where he'll be sleeping for a couple of years, we can really give him the once-over."

"Why the hell couldn't he have left me alone?" I said. "That was all I wanted."

"I know," said Boyson. "That's really all most of us want."

I didn't expect to see Sam down at the warehouse in the morning, but he was there when I arrived. He'd made coffee, and poured me a cup. We said good morning, and that's about all, except for details about the job.

"I got two of the coffee makers working," he said. "I think we can salvage six of them."

"Good," I said. "How about those soft drink coin mechanisms?"

"I put them on the workbench. I figured maybe you could combine parts and get maybe half of them in shape."

So that's what we did all morning. Reconstructed shattered parts, and said, politely, "Hand me that screwdriver," and deliberately ignored what had happened in court.

Around noon, he asked, "How are we doing?"

I said, "I estimate if we keep on like we're going, working day and night, we should have this place back to normal around April of nineteen eighty-five."

There was a long pause. Then he said, "Bill, I'm grateful for what you did. Trying to keep me out of it."

"Forget it," I said.

"I know you think I turned yellow. I don't blame you. But I had to give them what they wanted. You don't know the pressure I was under."

"I think I do," I said. "Remember Gus?"

"Yes," he said. "Well, maybe we're made of different stuff. I just couldn't stand up under it. I'm not proud of myself. But at least, now I don't have to go around looking over my shoulder. Let the law take care of Harry Cade. That's what we pay taxes for. I'm sorry for your trouble, Bill. But I still think you were a god-damned fool."

"Sam . . . do me a favor?"

"Sure."

"Let it drop, huh?"

We worked in silence. Then he said, "Do you think it's all over now?"

"That's what the D.A. thinks."

"Maybe we ought to hire a guard?"

I looked around at the wrecked warehouse. "With what? A case of Doctor Pepper?" I fumbled around the workbench. "Where the hell are those quarter-inch bolts?"

"We used them all up."

I pushed the box wrench away. "Great."

He got up. "I'll get some. We need anything else?"

I tossed him my keys. "Some sandwiches. And a six-pack. It's getting hot."

"You ought to cut down on the booze, Bill," he said, heading for the door.

I yelled after him, "And you ought to cut down on the advice."

He told me to go screw myself, and I grinned. Things were back to normal.

I worked for a moment. Then I heard the explosion.

You've heard how they say that time stands still? Well, it does. I was off that stool faster than I'd ever moved in my life, and out the door, and there it was, still bright orange and twisting in the air over the trees, and falling in balls of smoke—bits and pieces of my car broken into scrap. My eyes must have been playing tricks, because it was as if everything were in slow motion, and each separate movement was broken away from the preceding one, like those strobe light effects you find in some of the go-go discotheques. I do not remember even running toward the wreckage, but suddenly I was *there*, and the rumble of the explosion still filled my ears, and I was pawing through the burning metal, grabbing for Sam and calling his name, and his clothing was all aflame and I beat at the fire with my bare hands. I don't recall saying anything, but one of the firemen told me later that when they got there, I was crouched on the ground with Sam's charred body across my knees, rocking him back and forth and keening, "Oh, Sam, Sam, I'm sorry . . ."

NINE

YOU know about cemeteries.

The stone angels smiled down at us, smirking back the secret they alone know. The Madonnas eyed us compassionately, and the winged doves perched eternally on their marble twigs.

I detest funerals. But I couldn't avoid this one. I hadn't been invited—I hadn't even been able to reach Rita on the phone. She wasn't staying at the house, and I couldn't locate her. I only found out about the funeral by the notice in the newspaper.

The preacher was a real pro. I would have given you nine to five that he had never met Sam Morse in his life, but he came up with all the right words. I am not very conscious about religion, but I figured he was probably a Baptist. He was very big with the Judgment of God and the Resurrection.

There weren't that many people there. Rita, dressed in black, and her three children. Lucille and me. I'd called her, because I didn't want to show up alone. She refused at first, then called me back and said she would go, that she wanted to speak with me anyway. A couple of policemen—Boyson's goddamned inefficient protection squad. Although I knew I wronged him. Who can protect us when the dark forces gather? The mistake was in going against them to begin with. And the real guilt was mine.

The service wound up. Rita sprinkled a handful of earth into the grave, and it made a thumping sound on the coffin. The preacher was going from one member of the group to the next, clasping their hands and saying something in a low voice.

When he got up to me, he said it: "My son, have you been Saved?"

"Not exactly," I said. "I've got at least a dozen killers on my trail and I think they're closing in. Have you any ideas?"

His eyes went blank, and he moved on. That was fine with me. I had been afraid, for a moment, that there was a man behind that black suit and turned collar.

"Bill . . ." said Lucille reprovingly. It was what I expected.

I went over to Rita.

"I tried to call you before," I said. "But—"

She stared at me through the heavy black veil. "Bill," she said, "I don't want to talk with you now."

"You know how sorry I am—"

She laughed. I was surprised. It wasn't the sound you

figured to hear in a cemetery. But, then, it wasn't a pleasant laugh, either. She turned to the oldest of the three children. "Did you hear, Johnny?" she said. "He's *sorry*. Sarah, Paul—don't cry. He's *sorry*."

"Rita—"

She whirled on me. "What good does 'sorry' do?"

I spread my hands. "What can I say? I didn't intend for—"

She moved in close. "Why did you have to testify? He begged you not to. He was your *friend*, Bill. He admired you. He tried to protect you, but you wouldn't listen. You called him a coward, frightened by crank phone calls. He did everything he could to stop you, but you went right ahead." She put both hands against my chest and slowly pushed me away. "God damn you, William Kirby, *you* killed my Samuel, and I hope you rot in hell for it!"

Rita turned and walked away, followed by her three frightened children. I never saw any of them again.

I turned to Lucille. Numbly, I said, "How about that?"

She said, "She doesn't mean it." But her tone was flat, and gave the lie to her words.

"Not you too," I said.

"Yes, me too. Bill, I don't want you coming around to see Brian any more. Not until all this is settled."

"Now, wait just a damned minute—" I began.

"You wait a minute! Rita was right. This is *your* doing. I didn't ask for it, Brian didn't ask for it. Neither did poor Sam. It's all you, Bill, and we don't want any part of it. That poor woman was right. You're bad news. You're an accident looking for a place to happen. But not with Brian—not with my son!"

"We'll talk about this later," I said.

"I don't think so," she said. Then she turned and ran up the path.

As I left the cemetery gate, Harvey Baker, the man from the Justice Department, fell in step with me.

"Got a minute?" he asked.

"Sure," I growled. "Where the hell were you when we needed you?"

Instead of answering, he said, "Let's try to figure out how to save your life."

My knees almost went out from under me. Like they do when you step down an unexpected curb. We had just buried Sam Morse, but only now did it really hit hard. Stupidly, I said, "It's that bad?"

"That bomb was meant for you," Baker said.

It got me mad. "So what else is new?" I flared. "It seems to me I remember people telling me not to worry, they'd watch out for me. Who the hell was watching when those bastards were blowing Sam Morse into hamburger?"

He looked down at the path. "We goofed it. We were watching you, not your car. I'm sorry."

Furiously, I told him, "Mr. Baker, a beautiful, tragic lady said something to me this morning that I will never forget, and I am now going to pass it on to you and I hope *you* never forget it either. *What good does sorry do?*"

We were far down the hill from the cemetery. The tree-lined lane was moody with mist that was half rain. Why the hell does it always rain on funerals? I glanced over my shoulder. Two men were following us, remaining a discreet half-block behind. Their gray suits with narrow lapels were as distinctive as an army uniform. They might as well have been wearing blinking neon signs spelling out the word COP.

An ice cream wagon on a corner tinkled its jolly tunes and offered us nine flavors. I wondered how much this red-hot location had cost its operator.

Baker had said something that I hadn't heard. He tapped my arm.

"Mr. Kirby," he said. "This is important."

"Sorry. I was thinking about something else. What did you say?"

"Only repeating that we in Justice admit that we made a serious mistake. But look at our side, try to understand that there was nothing in Cade's past to suggest that he'd carry his hatred of you into a senseless, profitless vendetta. Those guys are usually sharper than that. They cut their losses."

"Why don't you say what you're getting around to?

What do you want from me now?"

"Mr. Kirby—Bill—we've got to put you underground."

I was on the thin edge. It seemed funny. I giggled. "You mean like good old Sam?"

"We have experience in this sort of thing. We've been hiding federal witnesses, informants, and so on, for quite a while. There's an entire task force set up for that purpose. Name change, Social Security numbers, army discharge, driver's license—the whole enchilada. They'll never find you."

I stopped in the middle of a crossing. A gravel truck honked at me and growled its gears. Baker grabbed my arm and hustled me up on the sidewalk.

"You want me to *what?*" I said.

"It's the only way we can assure your safety."

"Sell my business, what's left of it? Move away? Change my name? Give up my son?" I shook off his arm. "Like hell I will. No chance."

In a calm, level voice, he said, "It's your *only* chance. Bill, they won't let up now. You can go underground alive—or you can go underground dead. There's no third choice."

"But you represent the *government!* You know somebody's out to kill me. Christ, you've got the FBI, the army, the CIA! Do you mean to say the whole goddamned government can't stop a couple of hoods?"

"We don't know who they are," he said. "Sure, we

know Cade's behind it. But there's no proof. We can't move until they do. And that could be too late."

"So those killers go about their happy business while I dig a hole and crawl in? Who the hell runs this country, anyway?"

After a pause, he said, "That's a good question."

I didn't like the idea. Would you? But Baker was persuasive. Maybe I might be able to look out for myself, but what about Lucille and Brian?

"Once you're out of sight, they'll be all right," Baker assured me. "They don't go after a man's family. It's an unwritten law."

"You don't know how much that cheers me," I said bitterly. We were in his office downtown. I looked at my hands. They were shaking. "Okay, where do we start?"

"First, Bill, you've got to trust us completely. What's happening to you isn't unique. Probably you never heard of it, but the Crime Control Act of nineteen seventy gives the Justice Department authority to provide considerable aid to persons who testify in criminal cases. We're authorized to provide protection, compensation for losses—even new identities."

"How long would a new name last?" I said. "With those lousy computers everywhere, you could get nailed for an overdue library book."

"Not when we get through," Baker said. "Your name change will be a legal one. You'll have a new Social

Security number, even a completely new life history which will stand up to investigation. Of course, you have to relocate."

"Just like all those two-bit crooks who decided to rat on their buddies for immunity?"

He nodded. "You're right, Bill. Most of our cases *do* involve racketeers, or at any rate associates of racketeers. But not all of our 'protection and relocation' clients are like that. Some are victims. Maybe they've been ripped off by loan sharks, or harassed by gamblers or drug dealers. We call them 'innocent witnesses,' but they're entitled to our protection, too. And they get it. So far we've relocated more than a thousand witnesses in complete safety."

I gave him a hard look. "And you're *proud* of it? Too bad you didn't think of 'protection and relocation' in time to help Sam Morse."

He turned away. "Bill, you know how badly I feel about that. Why do you keep rubbing it in?"

"Because I'm goddamned mad!" I yelled. "That's why. I'm not the criminal, and Sam wasn't either. But somehow we end up paying the price. Hooray for your wonderful underground hideouts, but why should I have to resort to crap like that? Why the hell can't you keep those bastards off our backs?"

"We do the best we can," he said.

I snorted. "Well, if you want one man's opinion, that just ain't good enough."

He closed a folder on his desk and moved as if to get

up. I waved him back into his chair.

"Forget it. I'm all wound up," I told him. "What were you saying?"

"We have reason to believe that Harry Cade doesn't have syndicate approval for the attacks on you. But to be safe, we'll assume he has."

"My God," I interrupted. "This sounds just like a scene from *The Godfather*. So there really *is* a Mafia!"

"By that name and a dozen others."

"And all gunning for me."

He shook his head. "Maybe not. As I said, we think this is Cade's private revenge."

"Either way I go underground. Right?"

Slowly, he nodded. "For at least a year."

"That's the bottom line," I said. "What's the top?"

Reluctantly, he answered, "The rest of your life."

TEN

THE first interviewer was plump and bald and looked like a fag math teacher. Instead of writing on the card he held, he punched out little holes with the tip of a ball-point pen.

"Your Social Security number, please," he said.

"You mean national identity number, don't you?" I said sourly. "It's on every piece of paper I touch nowadays, including my driver's license."

"I mean your Social Security number," he said in the same neutral tone of voice.

"416–36–0847," I said, fast, hoping he would have to ask me to repeat it. He rubbed me wrong.

"Thank you," he said, unruffled. "How old were you when you received it?"

"Fourteen."

For the first time, his eyes met mine. They were cold and seemed to peer through me.

"That's very young," he said.

84

"I thought it would work as an I.D. so I could buy cigarettes."

The trace of a smile twitched at his lips. "Did it?"

"No," I said.

"That's good," he said, punching out two more holes on the card. "Cigarette smoking can be dangerous to your health."

"And the mortgage on the Peachtree View house has twelve years to run?"

"Unless she renews it," I said.

"How much are the payments?"

"One ninety a month." This interviewer had a small computer before him, and every number I gave him was punched into its digit-flashing-flicking face.

"What about your apartment?"

"That's a hundred ten. It's a twelve-month lease, with seven to go."

He punched in the numbers, then said, "I think we can get you out of the lease."

"Great," I said. "How about my key deposit?"

Blandly, he said, "That's between you and your landlord."

"Your top rank was sergeant?"

"Twice."

The interviewer's eyebrows raised.

"I got busted and had to work my way up again," I said.

"Were you court-martialed?"

"No. My Company commander caught me dating his sister."

"I find it hard to believe you were court-martialed for that."

"Well," I said, "we were dating his car, too, and neither one of us had thought to ask him."

"Any outstanding tax bills? Assessments? Liens?"

I considered this interviewer's question. I am always a little mixed up in the money department. Finally, I said, "I think the feds will probably get another three hundred for last year. But I'm still arguing with them."

He wrote that down.

"Hey," I said. "Does this mean I can forget about my buddies down at IRS?"

Without looking up from his form, he answered, "Not a chance."

"College?"

"University of Florida."

"Majoring in?"

"Blondes."

"Mr. Kirby, this is a serious matter."

"So are blondes. Or haven't you met the ex-Mrs. Kirby?"

"Please, sir."

"All right. Mechanical engineering."

"Thank you."

The next interviewer was a woman. It figures. Because she was the one assigned to explore my family life.

"Your ex-wife filed for the divorce?"

"You'd better believe it."

She overlooked the bitter anger in my voice. "Grounds?"

"She thought there were."

"I meant *what* grounds, Mr. Kirby."

I gave it a long beat. Then: "Adultery."

Now she hesitated. When she looked up, her eyes weren't hard at all, but seemed to be trying to see *me*, not just another case.

"Mr. Kirby, I'm sorry to ask you such personal questions. But we need their answers. They go into our closed files. No one can see them."

"Okay," I said.

"Was the charge true?"

Slowly, I said, "Yes. It was true."

At lunch in a small dining room off the cafeteria, Baker told me, "Our procedure for innocent witnesses is more complicated than just putting a former gangster underground. Such a case is happy to go along with anything he gets. He knows he's lucky to be in some out-of-the-way place, and he'll take any simple, undemanding job. All he's interested in is saving his life."

"This may come as a shock to you," I said, "but that happens to be on the top of my priority list, too."

"True," he said. "But later, when the shock wears off, you'll cause us problems unless we place you in the right environment, the right job, with access to the right life style."

"The voice of the expert," I said, finishing my coffee.

"So this afternoon you start your psychiatric counseling."

I nearly dropped the cup.

"A shrink? No, thanks."

Spooning up a chunk of peach ice cream, he said, "He's expecting you at two."

"You're a very lucky man, Mr. Kirby," said the shrink.

"How the hell do you figure that?"

He tapped his fingers on the desk between us. In this, my first visit to a real psychiatrist, as opposed to the Marine shrink who merely asked me if I liked girls, I was disappointed to find no trace of a leather couch anywhere in the room.

Carefully, he said, "Some of my patients come in here all swallowed up in guilt. They believe that they were fools to try to do the right thing, and that now their punishment is to be forced to move themselves and their families to a strange city under a strange name and start all over again from Square One."

"Funny," I said. "I may be very lucky, but that's exactly how I feel, too."

He gave a negative wave of his cigar. "Your case is far less severe than most, Mr. Kirby. You have already made your break with your family. You have no real ties in Atlanta, nothing close to hold you here. In the long run, you may find that this relocation will be the best thing that ever happened to you. It will give you new horizons, new challenges."

I got up. "Doc, are you at all interested in what *I* think?"

"Certainly. That's what we're here to find out."

"Well, I don't think you know your Freudian ass from a hole in the ground."

"Empty your pockets," said Baker.

I did, piling up the stuff on his desk. He sorted through it.

"Social Security card. Hunting license. Credit cards." He put them in a gray metal box. "We've already collected all your other important documents from your apartment and your safe deposit box."

"How did you get in that? The bank isn't supposed to let anyone but me touch it."

"The IRS has authority to open any safe deposit box in the country without notifying the owner. They help us out in cases like this."

"That's just great," I said. "Well, about that nine million dollars in unmarked bills. I can explain—"

He chuckled and slammed the little gray box closed. "Well, that's that."

I looked down at it. "That's what?"

"William Kirby is officially dead. Better than that, he never existed."

He handed me a heavy Manila envelope. I opened it. Inside were documents and identification cards. I leafed through them.

"They look real," I said.

"They *are* real. Your new passport, for instance. It was actually issued by the Department of State."

"Do they know it's a phony?"

"It's not a phony. Neither is your new Social Security number, or your driver's license, or any of those other papers. Even the Diner's Club computer has your new name, and you'll be happy to know you have an excellent credit rating."

I looked at the plastic card. It was made out to Kirby Grant. "You used half of my real name," I said.

"Right. That way, if somebody calls you by your new name before you get used to it, there's a good chance they'll say 'Kirby,' and you'll react correctly." He looked at his watch. "You're late for Indoctrination Drill."

"Are you sure I didn't see you in Miami?"

I stared at the interrogator. "I've never been to Miami."

"Where did you go to college?"

90

"Penn State."

"What was your major?"

"Blondes."

The interrogator threw down his pencil. "Mechanical engineering, damn it!"

"Okay. Blonde mechanical engineers."

"Kirby, in case you think this is a joke, it is not. Now, let's take it again from the top."

Patiently, I began to recite my new life. By now it had started becoming almost real, even to me. "When I got my discharge from the Air Force, I took the GI Bill and went to Pennsylvania, where I . . ."

I felt good when I came out of the tiny room. The last three drills had gone perfectly.

Waiting for the elevator, I lit a cigarette. Even these had been changed. Instead of Kents, I now smoked Pall Mall.

A guard, vaguely familiar, passed, reading from a clipboard. He put his finger against it, paused and called to me, "Hey, Bill."

I turned. "Yeah?"

He tossed the clipboard at me and while I was trying to keep it from hitting my head, the world went into slow motion as his hand dipped for his revolver. My mouth opened. I don't know what I was going to say, but I never got time anyway, because now the pistol was aimed directly at my belly and his finger was squeezing the trigger.

The echo of the shots rang up and down the corridor. The clipboard hit my shoulder and clattered to the floor. I stood there, petrified. I couldn't feel any pain.

Unbelievingly, I looked down. My hands felt my stomach—caressed my unwounded flesh. How could he have missed at this range?

Baker stepped out of an open doorway.

"God damn it," he yelled. "Your name is Kirby! Kirby Grant! Remember that."

The guard holstered his gun. He grinned at me. "Blanks," he said.

Weakly, I said, "You made your point."

ELEVEN

THAT evening, Baker drove me downtown to Jimmy Orr's Restaurant. On the way in, we saw Hank Aaron coming out.

"This is pretty public for a guy who's supposed to be hiding out," I said.

Baker grinned. "You can't see them, but we're well covered by security men."

"Just like Bobby Kennedy?"

"You have a certain abrasiveness, Kirby, that is hard to learn to enjoy."

"Who invited you?"

Inside, we sat down under the big photographs of sports greats and had a drink.

"What's the occasion?" I asked.

"This is your graduation," Baker said. Lifting his glass, he added, "Good luck."

"Thanks," I said. We drank.

A deep voice at my elbow inquired, "Mr. Baker?"

I pointed at Baker. "That's him."

The voice had come from a big, shaggy man whose brown tweed jacket matched the color of his briar pipe.

"Noodle?" asked Baker.

"Right," said Shaggy.

"Noodle?" I said. "What the hell kind of name is that?"

Noodle said, "I feel the same way. I don't know what joker thinks up these code identities, but he ought to work for Sid Caesar."

"Sit down," said Baker. "Kirby, Noodle's a U.S. marshal."

"Great," I said. "What's your real name, since we're friends?"

Baker held up his hand. "Even I'm not allowed to know it," he said.

"You're not what? I thought you ran this outfit."

"Mr. Grant," said Noodle, "I know this sounds like The Man from U.N.C.L.E., but it's serious business. I don't know your real name, and I never will. It's my job to relocate you and to act as liaison between you and the Justice Department."

"I'll be goddamned," I said. "Is this for real?"

"It's very real, Kirby," said Baker. "The purpose for all this is to be sure that nobody—and that means *no* body—in Atlanta or even Washington has any idea where you've relocated."

"Nobody but Noodle," I said.

"That's right," said the shaggy man. "I'll forward your mail, I'll see your old bills get paid. If you have to yell at anyone, you yell at me."

"But what about my family—my boy?"

"You can write as often as you want. I'll forward the letters to Baker, who readdresses them and sends them on."

"After censoring them, no doubt," I said.

Noodle gave me a slow smile. "No," he said. "We rely on your own sense of self-preservation to keep you from committing postal suicide."

"When do I see them?"

"Whenever you want, within reason. We arrange meetings at safe, neutral locations. Naturally we have to be sure they aren't followed."

"I just don't believe you guys," I mumbled.

Noodle leaned forward. "You'd better believe us, Kirby. Your life depends on it."

While we were packing up the next day, my old buddy Harry Cade had a visit from his lieutenant, Tony D'Amato. They faced each other through a double glass window and spoke through directly connected telephones.

"What the hell do you mean, you can't find him?" yelled Cade.

"He ain't been to work for a week," said D'Amato. "He hasn't come home to his apartment, but somebody moved his stuff out. He don't even go to see his kid any more."

"He's got to be somewhere," said Cade. "He doesn't have the kind of bread that would let him just bug out. Put some more muscle on the street. Find that fink."

D'Amato hesitated. "Harry," he said, "I hate to be the one to tell you, but—"

"But what?"

"Well, the truth is the boys don't think this guy is all that important. I mean, to put on so much heat."

Cade leaned forward. "Did they cancel my contract on him?"

"No," D'Amato said. "Not straight out. But—"

"Then that's it," said Cade. "Put out the word. Five grand to anybody who finds Kirby and wastes him."

And, later that night, other people were having trouble finding me, too.

Noodle yelled into the phone, "Where the hell is Kirby? We're supposed to leave tonight, and he's gone."

At the other end of the connection, Harvey Baker groaned. "And here I thought I was rid of him. I should have warned you, Kirby sometimes does things his own way. All right, stay there at the motel. I think I know where to find him."

Where I was, at that moment, could only have been seen by a bird perched in the giant live oak behind my house—I guess I should say my ex-wife's—on Peachtree View. I went up its branches quietly. Brian and I had often used this escape route to get out for a fishing expedition without being seen by front parlor company.

The light in his bedroom was out, but the window was ajar. I opened it all the way and slipped in.

He must have been awake. I heard him sit up, the light came on, and he said, "Who's there?"

"Shhh," I said. "It's me. Daddy."

He jumped out of the bed and ran over to me. He was wearing those stupid Atlanta Braves pajamas I gave him last Christmas. "Daddy!" he yelped.

"Hold it down," I hissed. "We don't want to wake your mother."

"Oh," he whispered. "Okay."

I hugged him. "How you been, buddy?"

"Fine," he said. "But I m-m-missed you."

"Me too," I said. "Caught any good fish lately?"

He shook his head. "We don't go out much. Mom's awful worried about something."

"Well, don't let her get down in the dumps," I said. "I can depend on you, right?"

"Right," he said very seriously.

"And I want you to keep a secret. Promise?"

"Promise," he repeated.

"Well, son, I'm going to have to go away for a while."

His lip trembled. "For a long time?"

"I don't know. I hope not. But I won't be able to see you or even phone."

He stared down at the floor. "Gee," he said.

"But I'll write, Brian. I'll write you every week."

He looked at me, his eyes wide. "Daddy, does this have s-s-something to do with those men who messed up the warehouse?"

"Sort of," I said. "But don't worry, Brian. Everything's going to be fine."

"Where are you going?"

I shook my head. "It's a secret."

"Oh." A pause. "When will you be back?"

"As soon as I can. You know that."

"But w-w-when?"

I hugged him again. "No later than Christmas. I promise."

"Daddy, are you *sure?*"

"I'm sure," I said, wondering if I were.

He followed me to the window. I bent down and kissed his cheek. His arms tightened around my neck. After a while, I pulled them free. "So long, Brian. You hang in there, buddy, y'hear?"

I didn't look back as I went out the window, so I didn't see Lucille standing in the darkened hallway, tears glistening on her cheeks.

Harvey Baker was waiting in his car. He leaned out and scared me out of a year's growth.

"Goddamn it, Kirby, get in! You're late."

I slipped into the front seat. "How did you find me?"

He snapped my head back starting off down Peachtree. "Idiot! If I'm smart enough to figure you'd come here, don't you think Cade's men are just as smart?"

"Don't nag," I said. But I checked behind us anyway. "Nobody's following," I told him.

"No thanks to your brains," he grumbled. "It's good you're lucky."

"Unlucky at love, lucky at everything else."

I was wrong, of course. Although nobody had followed us, a slim, dark man stood in the shadows of the driveway writing down Baker's license number.

Baker delivered me to Noodle's motel, where I was hustled into a waiting station wagon filled with my suitcases, and we were off to the airport. I didn't get a look at the tickets, but I noticed that the plane we boarded was going to Memphis.

I stared out the window during takeoff. The lights tilted and fell below as the city receded.

Imitating Jackie Gleason, I muttered, "And away-y-y we go."

Noodle said, "Kirby, are you really a funny guy? Or is it all just noise?"

I leveled with him. "Noodle, if I didn't manage to keep myself laughing, you would hear weeping and wailing that would bust your eardrums."

"That's what I figured," he said sympathetically. "I don't blame you. This is a rough deal."

"Have you handled many of them? Relocations?"

He shook his head. "We're virgins together. This is my first time, too."

I sighed. "Well, I hope I like Memphis."

He laughed. "Cheer up, it isn't that bad."

"No, it *could* have been St. Louis."

"Well, smile. It's not Memphis."

"Where, then?"

"New Orleans. We're doubling back from Memphis just to confuse the track."

"New Orleans," I said. "Well, why not?"

"It's a nice town," said Noodle.

"Sure," I said. "If you like Dixieland music and red beans and rice."

While I was being flip and clever with Noodle, Tony D'Amato was talking with Harry Cade again.

"We had the license number traced by a friend in the MVB," he reported. "It's registered to a lawyer named Baker."

"Kirby's mouthpiece?"

"No. He works for the Justice Department."

"Great," said Cade. "I remember now. That bastard in court." He leaned forward, sweat rolling down his jowled cheeks. "Tony, get on the stick. Move! They're pulling the stash on us. Find that fink before they hide him."

"Harry . . ."

"What?"

"Why is this Kirby guy so different? You always rolled

with the punches before. What's wrong now? Why are you so mad?"

Cade said, "Tony, I gave him money. I handed him *money,* and he still set me up. I can't let some civilian do that to me."

"No," Tony said. "I guess not."

"Find him!" Cade said, almost pleading. "Get your ass moving, Tony, and locate Kirby!"

Part Two
NEW ORLEANS

ONE

THE New Orleans you see in Mardi Gras movies and plays by Tennessee Williams really exists, but it does so side by side with the hard world of commerce, and that's the world I found myself in. Noodle had rented me an apartment on the edge of the French Quarter, but he warned me that I probably wouldn't like it.

"Then why did you set it up?" I asked.

"Because if I put you where you belong, out in Gretna, or in Gentilly Woods, you'd be bitching about how you wanted to live in the Quarter. This way you can get it out of your system. Who knows? You might like it. Some people don't mind listening to drunks staggering past their window all night."

"Some ambassador you are," I said.

He looked at his watch. "Your stuff is already there." He gave me the address. "Any cab'll get you to the right place."

"Aren't you coming along?"

"We shouldn't be seen together any more than absolutely necessary."

"What if you're right and I hate the apartment?"

"Move out. You're not a prisoner. Just keep me posted where you are." He gave me two cards. "This one is my private number. The other one, Gaskin, Inc., is where we've got a job lined up for you."

"Fast work."

He shrugged. "We keep up our contacts with certain firms around the country. They're glad to help us out."

"Particularly when and if they might need a favor from the Justice Department?"

He gave me a slow wink. Well, why not? One hand washes the other.

I took a cab, found the address of my apartment at the corners of North Claiborne and Orleans Streets. It was too early in the day to tell about the drunks, but Noodle hadn't mentioned that I would have a superb view of Interstate Highway 10 cutting between the century-old buildings on its way to Baton Rouge.

Someone had stocked the refrigerator with cans of Jax beer. I opened one, stared out the window toward the Mississippi River, and sipped at it.

I didn't allow myself to think of Brian. But I missed Gus.

New Orleans is very proud of its Superdome, deliberately built to dwarf the Houston Astrodome. The residents wince a little when reminded that its construction was scandal-ridden, and that indictments are still being handed down for hanky-pank in bids and payments.

But the building itself is magnificent. Instead of planting it in the outskirts of town, where most new arenas are located, the builders carved out an area hundreds of yards square and plunked the Superdome down alongside Canal Street. It squats like a plump flying saucer, surrounded by parking lots, right in the heart of the city.

Gaskin, Inc., turned out to be one mobile home set up in a corner of Lot B, on the east side of the Superdome.

The trailer was split into two offices. I stood in the outer one and introduced myself to the secretary who handled the phone, typed at a letter, and talked to me —more or less simultaneously.

"I'm Kirby Grant," I said. "I have an appointment with Mr. Gaskins."

She gave a bob of her cute, brunette head to let me know she'd heard, pleaded with someone on the other end of the phone to get on the stick and deliver some wiring, pulled the letter from her IBM Selectric, and hit a button on the desk with her elbow.

The door to the inner office opened and a heavy-set man wearing a blue western shirt, jeans and high-heeled cowboy boots came out. He was in his fifties, and his sunburned face looked as if someone had once walked on it with golf shoes.

"Kirby?" he boomed. "Come on in." As I followed him, he called over his shoulder, "Judy, no calls."

She bobbed her head again and pleaded once more for wiring.

Gaskins shut the door.

"I want to thank you, Mr. Gaskins—" I began.

He motioned me to a chair near the big roll-top desk that was out of place in the modern interior of the trailer. "Gaskins was my paw's name. Most folks call me Hoss. Real name's George, but I don't like that much neither." He studied me. "Well. You come with mighty high recommendations, Kirby."

Carefully, I said, "I hope they didn't oversell me."

He bellowed a laugh. "Put your mind at rest. I know the score. But don't you worry none. Nobody, and that means *no*body but me and that government man who got you this job knows you ain't exactly what your personnel record says you are. Not even Judy." He jerked his head toward the outer office. "And that's the way it's gonna stay."

"Thanks," I said, not knowing what else to say.

George "Hoss" Gaskins didn't seem to hear me. He kept rolling on like the mighty Mississippi itself. "That government man, he told me you done a good thing for our country that he couldn't mention, and would I take you on, no questions asked. What kind of American would I be if I'd said 'No'?"

Embarrassed, I said, "What kind of job did you have in mind for me?"

"Hell, boy, no sweat. You won't have the least bit of trouble, not with your training."

"It's been a long time since college, Mr.—Hoss. I may need a brush-up."

"Naw, we're right up your alley. Didn't they tell you what line we're in?"

"Not exactly."

"I'm putting in a whole new batch of vending machines. The Superdome Commission decided they weren't getting enough return on the ones they had before."

I guess the disappointment showed on my face. I hadn't exactly been looking forward to going right back into the business I had so recently left.

Hoss Gaskins misread it. He punched me on the arm. "Look, you won't always be just on wages. You work out, there'll be a piece of the action for you."

I forced a grin. "That's what I like to hear. Okay, what do I do first?"

He poked a bananalike finger at a blueprint. "You see all them public johns on the third level?"

I saw them and nodded.

Hoss grinned as if he had just discovered gold. "Well, I got us an okay to install two dozen condom machines in there. So get right on it."

I had to go to the telephone company during lunch to put a deposit down. I discovered that along the Gulf Coast the utilities aren't as trusting as they were in

Atlanta. I had to fork out fifty bucks to get a number. And answer a lot of questions.

The clerk asked, "Did you ever have a phone before, Mr. Grant?"

I hesitated. "Yes—I mean—"

"Yes or no."

"Well . . . yes."

"Where?"

Without thinking, I said, "Atlanta." I stood there then, my mouth gaping, wishing I could call the word back.

The clerk didn't notice. She kept on filling out the form. Without looking up, she said, "All right, sir. It may take us a day or so to hook you up. We're short of instruments. The energy crisis, you know."

The energy crisis, I had noticed for the past couple of years, was responsible for almost everything that went wrong.

I got my mouth closed. The clerk looked up. "Is there anything else, sir?"

"Uh—about Atlanta," I said. "Could I have that form back?" It was all I could do to keep from tearing it out of her hands. Careful, I warned myself. You mustn't attract any more attention than you have already.

"Beg pardon?" she said.

"I made a mistake. Tear that form up. I never had a phone in Atlanta."

"I'm sorry, sir," she said, putting the form down on

the desk far out of my reach. "I'm not allowed to destroy an application."

"But—about Atlanta. It's wrong."

Without realizing how her words relieved my fear, she said, "I didn't write that down anyway. We never check out of state."

The telephone installation man was waiting for me when I got home from work, glowering at his watch and at me.

"I was just getting ready to leave," he grumbled.

So much for the energy crisis.

TWO

Lonely is lonely, no matter where you are.

New Orleans is a great place to be lonely. Tropic in attitude, if not quite so in climate, the city life spills out onto the wrought-iron balconies and cobbled streets.

Like Greenwich Village—and Underground Atlanta, for that matter—the French Quarter is a tourist rip-off. Even so, it can be fun.

It can also be bone-aching lonely.

Al Hirt, the big bearded trumpet player, has a joint on Bourbon Street, just a couple of blocks away from the Playboy Club. I am not much for Playboy Clubs, although I carry a "key" card (which is made of metal and invariably sets off the anti-hijacking metal detectors at airports). So I opted for Al Hirt's club, picking my way between throngs of happy merrymakers, weaving up and down Bourbon Street carrying "walkaway cocktails" and swigging from them on every corner. New Orleans is the only city I've ever been in where it seems to be legal to imbibe anywhere you happen to be—street corner, store lobby, supermarket—you name it. It must be the French influence.

At the bar, I said, "Mint julep." Might as well go the whole route.

"Sorry," said the bartender, beaming a great smile at me from his shining black face. "No mint."

"No mint?"

"Out of season," he said.

"Give me a beer then."

As he went to get it, I turned to a long-legged blonde girl two stools away and said, "Can you believe that?"

She gave me a big smile. "Mint's always out of season on Saturday night. Anywhere in the Quarter."

I moved over one stool to be near her. She met my eyes and the smile remained. Ah, Kirby, you gay dog. Good-bye to the blues.

"Why's that?" I asked.

"It takes too long to mix up a mint julep. The bars want to keep turning those glasses over."

"That sounds reasonable," I said, wondering if she were putting me on. My beer came. "Can I buy you a drink? Anything but a mint julep, that is?"

She indicated what appeared to be a Scotch and water. "No, thanks. I'm still working on this."

The ice was almost melted. She had obviously been working on it for quite some time. Maybe she was a jazz freak, sitting at the bar to hear Al Hirt instead of getting drunk and/or laid.

I sipped my beer. It was cold and frothy. "Do you live in New Orleans?" I asked.

"Mobile."

I stared at her. "Alabama," she added.

"I know where it is," I said, "It's just that—well, that's quite a drive."

"I always come over for the weekend," she said, still looking into my eyes. Was there a challenge there?

I decided to make the play. "Where are your friends?" I asked.

"What friends?" she said.

I gave her my loose, Paul Newman smile. What the hell, it always worked on the Atlanta co-eds. "It's my impression that all good-looking girls from Mobile always arrive with two other females in tow. Safety in numbers and all that."

She picked up the invitation. "Maybe," she said, still smiling, "I'm not looking for safety."

Bingo. I let Paul Newman blend into a little cruel Yul Brynner. "Well," I said. "You came to the right place. My name's Kirby."

"Nancy," she said.

"With the laughing face?"

"What?" she asked, losing a half inch of the smile.

"Just a song Frank Sinatra sang for his daughter Nancy a long time ago."

"I guess you're making a joke, huh?" said Nancy from

114

Mobile hesitantly. How old was she? Twenty-five? No college girl, anyway. Her mouth was a little too wide, and her eyes wore false lashes that could have impaled you. But she was cute.

"Yeah," I said. "I guess so."

The bartender was back. "Two more?"

I looked at Nancy. She gave a slight shake of her head.

"No, thanks," I said, paying up. He only took out for the beer. Nancy with the laughing face had already paid for her own, it seemed.

We dragged Bourbon Street.

Sipping walkaway Sazeracs we bought in the Old Absinthe Bar at 400 Bourbon: "Do you come over to New Orleans often?"

"Every weekend."

"Oh, right. You said that. Why?"

Nancy stopped near an old, leaning lamppost and sipped at her Sazerac. "Have you ever been to Mobile?"

"No."

"Well, if you had, you'd know."

In Your Father's Mustache, a noisy place with decor of the early 20's. Banjo players were having at Scott Joplin's "The Entertainer" with verve.

"This kind of music's just catching on, isn't it?" Nancy said. "I mean since that movie, *The Sting*?"

"Yeah," I said. "Since around nineteen ten."

115

Nancy giggled, drinking beer from a mustache cup. "You're putting me on."

"Or vice versa," I said.

In the Playboy Club:

Nancy, staring at white, fluffy bunny tails: "You'd think they'd catch cold."

"The tail keeps them warm," I said.

Midnight, wandering up St. Ann Street, along the edge of Jackson Square: "Now what?"

I shrugged. "Some coffee? We could go to my apartment."

Her fingers tightened on my arm.

"I thought you'd never ask," she said, brushing her warm lips against my cheek.

Dawn. I stared down at the traffic on I–10. Nancy was dozing. I was wide awake.

"Sorry," I'd said.

She had tried to comfort me. "It's all right, Kirby. You just had too much to drink."

"Sure. That must be it."

No breakfast. She decided to catch the early bus. I took her down to the Trailways station. She didn't offer her last name or phone number, and I didn't ask.

"Well," I said as the driver waited impatiently. She

was the last passenger to board. "If you ever get back to New Orleans . . ."

"Right," she said with false brightness. "I'll call. You're in the book."

"I'm in the book," I said.

"Bye-bye," she said, starting up the bus steps.

"So long," I said.

Trailways took her away. I choked in the exhaust fumes and watched the bus make its turn into traffic.

Then I walked back to the apartment.

Not for one single second, all night, had the aching loneliness ever left me.

THREE

A WEEK went by. I called Noodle's private number on Friday, expecting to hear some operator say "Justice Department," or something. Instead, his voice came on—flat, noncommittal.

"Noodle."

"Kirby. You forget about me?"

"No."

"Where's my mail you were supposed to forward?"

"Sorry, Kirby. Nothing's come."

I swore. He said, "Look, I don't write them. I just forward them. Maybe tomorrow."

I swore some more. He asked, "How's the job coming?"

"Great," I said. "I started on condom machines, but I think they're going to let me work up to comb dispensers."

"You don't sound happy."

"Oh? Am I supposed to have all this and be happy

too? I apologize, Noodle. I didn't know."

He didn't answer for a while. Then he said, "Is there anything else?"

"Yeah," I said. "How do I get a transfer out of this chicken outfit?"

He didn't laugh.

There wasn't much to laugh about anywhere, as it turned out. That was the morning Tony D'Amato turned up at Atlanta Federal Penitentiary and reported to Harry Cade, who blew his cork.

Cade shouted, "Fifteen soldiers on the street and you can't turn up one lousy fink?"

"Harry, he's not *there*," D'Amato said. "They must have buried him. I bet they pulled a relocation."

Cade thought about that for a moment. "Yeah," he said. "You pegged it." He made a decisive movement. "Cancel the contract."

"Call off the hit?"

"You heard me."

D'Amato wiped sweat from his forehead. "Harry," he said, "I'm glad to hear you say that. Because to tell the truth, the boys—"

"Screw the boys," said Cade. "Listen close, Tony. I want you to get hold of the Bookkeeper."

D'Amato drew back. "But, Harry—"

"Don't you hear so good? I want to talk to the Book-keeper."

119

"The boys won't like that, Harry—"

"The boys ain't pulling hard time in here. Do what I said, Tony. You understand?"

Slowly, D'Amato nodded. "I understand," he said unhappily.

I'd never heard of the Bookkeeper, of course. Harvey Baker had, but Harvey Baker didn't know that Cade had sent for him. So, while I installed condom machines in the Superdome's public johns, the word spread westward from the Atlanta Federal Penitentiary until it reached a faded redwood beachhouse near Big Sur, California.

If Baker had hit the right computer buttons, a card would have spewed out down at the National Crime Commission's files bearing the photograph of a slim, undistinguished man of thirty-five, identified as "Luke Martin also known as 'The Bookkeeper.' " Coded references would have revealed that while he had never been convicted—or even formally arrested—that Luke Martin had earned a reputation as the most successful hit man in organized crime.

But Baker didn't press the button.

When Luke Martin received the phone call, he was engaged in putting the finishing touches on a sandpiper which was mounted, stuffed, on a chunk of driftwood. Taxidermy was Luke's passion, and of course he killed all his own specimens. His large living room was a giant museum of once-living fauna.

Baker's card would also have listed Luke Martin's credentials as "graduate—Harvard School of Business. Certified Public Accountant." These were standard notations on the card. The designation of "killer" would have had to be written in by the computer's word retriever.

Orphaned at nine through an automobile accident that left him in the custody of his maternal aunt, Luke Martin had spent an uneventful childhood, distinguished only by his facility with mathematics. He earned a scholarship at M.I.T., but left after a few months in an unusual transfer directly to Harvard, arranged by a professor there who was most impressed with Luke's keen sense of business and economics. His talents included an uncanny instinct for which way the stock market was going to move, and by graduation he had a small but active portfolio working for him on the Street.

Maybe he would have gone on to become another of the quiet, unpublicized millionaires who avoid notice—and the IRS—by being grayly quiet and blending into the background. But, by accident, he became immersed in the world of organized crime.

Luke must have suspected that one of his clients, a shipping expediter, was anything but legal. But the numbers on the ruled pages—and their manipulation—were all that interested him.

Then, returning to his client's office one night, Luke Martin walked into a scene of violence that would change his life forever.

He found the shipping expediter standing over the body of a man, holding a smoking revolver, while a second man huddled in a corner, hands over his face.

The killer turned to Luke, the gun ready . . . recognized him. For a second, Luke was a breath away from death. Then the killer recognized something on Luke's face that kept his finger from pulling the trigger.

It was a rapt, almost sexual fascination caused by the scene of bloody death.

Slowly, the killer handed Luke the pistol and jerked his head toward the man in the corner.

"Him," he said.

Luke raised the gun. He was at the watershed of his life.

He pulled the trigger. The man in the corner screamed and clutched at his neck, where the bullet had struck.

Luke fired again—and again, until the pistol was empty. The last three bullets smashed into the body of a man who was already dead.

Luke Martin had finally found what he'd been searching for all his life.

Down New Orleans way, us working types get Wednesday afternoons off and make up for it by going in for Saturday morning. I did.

Judy Taylor, Hoss Gaskins' receptionist, gave me a wry look as I punched in.

"Sour taste?" I asked.

"You're late," she said.

"I'll leave early to make up for it."

"Don't joke. He's pretty mad."

I looked at the time clock. It was eight-forty. So I was ten minutes late.

"Big deal," I said. "Did one of his rubber machines get clogged up?"

I heard his voice bellow through the closed door between the two areas of the mobile home. "Judy! Is that Kirby out there?"

Without punching the button of the intercom, she yelled back, "Yes!"

"What did Hoss spend good money on that gadget for if you never use it?" I asked.

She shook her head and pleaded, with her eyes, for me to take it easy.

I went in without knocking.

"Banker's hours, Mr. Grant?" Hoss snarled.

"Sorry. I hit traffic."

He jabbed his finger at the ever-present blueprint. "What the hell's going on up there on the second level? You should have been finished by now. Don't you realize I have to pay overtime to those goddamned electricians?"

"Hoss, have you ever been up there?"

"Mr. Gaskins to you, and hell yes I've been up there. I've been all over this lousy dome."

"Well, if you saw what the second level's like, why

123

did you order vending machines three inches too wide to fit in the space allotted to them?"

He made a choking sound. "Those are the right machines," he said. "Listen, boy, I been up there this morning already while you were laying around in your fancy apartment. Do you know why those machines wouldn't fit? Do you want me to tell you why?"

"I know why," I said. "You got the wrong size."

He shoved the blueprint at me. "Take a good look, Kirby." He jabbed at the blue and white paper with a work-scarred finger. "This is where you were supposed to put them. And *this*"—jabbing at another spot—"is where you tried to squeeze them in. Goddamnit, you were working in the wrong area!"

I stared at the blueprint. He was right.

I mumbled an apology. He didn't seem to hear it.

His voice was surly. "Look, Grant," he said, "we both know you're a special case. But, boy, you still got to *do* the job. I can't pay you if you dog it."

"I made a mistake," I said. "I apologize. But I'm not dogging anything."

"You can't just sit back and figure we *owe* you a living because once upon a time you did something to get you in good with Washington, Dee Cee—"

It hit a raw spot. "Damn it!" I flared. "Shut up."

His hands closed, tensed. For a moment I thought he was going to swing on me. I got ready, but knew I didn't have a chance.

Then he relaxed.

124

"Kirby," he said softly, "I am going to forget you ever said that. I'm going to give you one more try. Maybe if you put in some overtime today, we can get back on schedule even if we go over budget. Do you think you could arrange that little thing for me?"

"I'll do the overtime," I said. "And you don't have to pay me. It was my mistake."

"That's mighty big of you," he said without a smile. "I don't suppose you'd be interested in picking up the bill those electrician guys are going to send me, too?"

I couldn't answer. I turned and left.

In California, Luke Martin's telephone had rung, he answered it, packed and got on an airplane.

Now he spoke through a double thickness of glass to Harry Cade.

"Fifty big ones," Cade said, holding up five stubby fingers.

Calmly, the Bookkeeper said, "For a down payment. Fifty more when I get him."

"You're off your head!" Cade yelled. "No hit's worth a hundred grand."

Luke Martin started to get up. Frantically, Cade waved him back to his chair.

"Wait!" Cade said. "Listen, that's awful stiff."

The Bookkeeper said, "This is no ordinary hard contract. You and your stumblebums have fouled it up beyond belief. Before I can hit Kirby, I've got to locate him. Do you know how hard that's going to be now?

The Justice Department has had all the time in the world to hide him where nobody but me has a chance in hell of finding him. And even for me, it's not going to be easy. Cade, they've submarined him."

Bitterly, Cade said, "So tell me something I don't already know. Why do you think I sent for you?"

Luke went on, "Furthermore, your own partners are none too pleased with this contract. Their feeling is that you've overreacted. Instead of expecting help from them, I may get trouble."

"All right," Cade said. "You got me by the short hairs. Fifty now, fifty more when you score."

"Very well," said Luke Martin. He stood up.

Cade motioned for him to pick up the telephone again.

"Yes?" said Luke.

"Bookkeeper," said Harry Cade, "how the hell are you going to find Kirby, anyway?"

"That, Mr. Cade," said Luke, "is my business."

FOUR

LUKE Martin didn't waste any time. He paid a visit to Tony D'Amato and collected his advance payment. He counted it, too.

D'Amato counted along with him. "Forty-nine. Fifty. It's all there."

The Bookkeeper put the bills in an envelope and slipped it into his pocket. "You don't seem too happy about this," he said.

"Why should I be?" D'Amato said. "This is clean money. It's Harry's Go-South dough. No heat, no laundering, no questions asked. So what are we spending it on? A crummy little hit that nobody gives a damn about."

"Nobody," said the Bookkeeper, "except Harry Cade."

Anxiously, D'Amato said, "Make it look like an accident, will you? The boys don't want any more heat. They're not any too happy with Harry as it is."

"That's Harry's problem," said Luke Martin. He

looked at his watch. "You're sure you'll have the other fifty."

"Harry's got it stashed," said D'Amato. "When I tip him that you've scored, he'll tell me where it is."

"He wouldn't develop a sudden case of amnesia by any chance?"

D'Amato made an angry gesture. "You know better than that. Harry never welshed in his life."

"All right," said the Bookkeeper, standing. "I'll be in touch."

D'Amato followed him to the door. "Listen," he pleaded, "like I said. Make it look like an accident."

In the New Orleans Superdome, I had a genuine accident of my own. My mind wandered, I found myself thinking of Brian, and before I knew what had happened, I had shorted a screwdriver across a pair of hot leads and blew the guts out of a two-thousand-dollar coin changing machine.

Hoss Gaskins didn't say a word when I told him. He just shook his head. But when I left the office, he picked up the phone, dialed a number and, when it was answered, said, "Mr. Rizzo? Hoss Gaskins. Listen, I know I said I'd help, but that feller of yours, Kirby Grant, he just ain't working out."

"What's wrong?" asked Noodle.

"I don't know. It's like his heart ain't in it. He walks around on a cloud. I hate to say it, but I'm going to have to let him go."

"I understand," said Noodle. "Well, thanks for your help anyway."

"Sure thing," said Hoss, and hung up. Then he called out to Judy and told her to have me report to him at the end of the day.

Noodle chewed me out, but he was sympathetic.

"Maybe I can do something with my hands," I said. "Outdoors."

We were driving along the north shore. He jerked his head toward the docks, clustered on the edge of Lake Pontchartrain. We had just passed the 26-mile causeway. "How about boats?"

"Hauling in shrimp nets? I wouldn't last an hour."

He turned in toward the city yacht harbor. "I was thinking more in the area of sports fishing."

I grinned. "You bastard, you've already got it set up, haven't you?"

"Let's say it was merely a contingency safety valve. Do you think you might be happier?"

"It's worth a try," I said.

The boat was named *Marie II,* the captain was a tough, wiry little Cajun named Landau, and he had an accent that sounded like a mixture between tough Brooklynese and hearty Gaelic. He'd greeted Noodle with warm friendship, gripped my hand in what felt like a bear trap, and now that Noodle had gone, stood on the dock staring at me and shaking his shaggy head.

129

It's impossible to reproduce in writing the Cajun patois. Landau never used the right word when he could transform it into something else by adding syllables that sounded right until you analyzed them. For instance, a shotgun became a shootgun, and wonderful —a word he seldom had occasion to use—evolved into wondermous.

"That" became "dat," final "t"s were dropped with abandon—don' for don't, and many "h"s vanished, too.

So, as Captain Landau stared at me and growled what I took to be a complaint, I heard, "How you like dat? You don' look so hot to me. I can see avery pinky finger from r'at chere."

I looked down at my fingers. They looked all right to me.

"What's the matter with them?" I asked.

"Ma' frien' tole me dat dis fallow frien' of his, dass you, come wid experience." He glowered at me. "Can you tole me dat?"

"I know about fishing," I said. "And some about motors. But I'm not a professional boatman."

He shook his head sadly. "You don' gone lass, but less go anyhow."

He was nearly right. Sports fishing may be fun for the clients, but it's hell on the mate, which was me. Between landing writhing sea trout, baiting hooks, swabbing blood off the deck, untangling lines and fighting against seasickness, I nearly gave up before sundown.

130

When we tied up, I cleaned out the fish for the clients, went over the brightwork with a cloth, pumped out the bilges, checked the lines, then climbed unsteadily up to the dock.

Landau stood spread-legged, hands on his hips, glowering at me.

"Okay," I said. "I get the message. Thanks for the boat ride. You don't have to bother paying me."

To my surprise, he gave me a big smile. "Kirby, I feel so sorry fo' you dis day I don' know w'at to did."

"I guess you were right. I didn't come with any experience."

"No, you did not dat. But you don' give up. W'at say we take ourself down to dat barroom saloon an' get damn dronk, I ga-ron-TEE."

Landau was as good as his word. We wrapped ourselves around a full case of beer and I barely got home, I guarantee.

I had lunch next day with Noodle and gave him a letter to forward to Atlanta.

"For Brian?" he asked.

I nodded.

"I'll get it out this afternoon," he promised.

"Nothing's come in?"

He shook his head. "Sorry."

I bit my lip. "What the hell's wrong with Lucy!" He made no comment.

Over coffee, he asked, "How's the new job going?"

"Pretty good," I said, holding my hands out for him to examine.

"Blisters?"

"Blisters on blisters. I got a shark today. On a hand line."

He whistled. "Wish I could have seen that."

"Why don't you come out with us one day? Cap Landau told me I could bring friends any time the schedule's light."

"No," he said. "I couldn't do that."

"Afraid of blowing my cover?"

He patted his stomach. "Afraid of getting seasick."

That afternoon, the *Marie II* and I both got a surprise. The party of four which had booked it included Judy Taylor, Hoss Gaskins' secretary. She didn't seem surprised to see me, but she didn't let on that she knew me, either. Two of the party were Tim and Betty Sharp, a tourist couple from Memphis. Judy's companion was named Charlie, and I didn't get his last name. He was well dressed, very sure of himself, and probably sold refrigerators to Eskimos. It was hate at first sight between us.

The day was fiercely hot, and Charlie had more than his share of beer during the long run out to the Mississippi Sound where we began trolling for mackerel or kingfish, or anything that would hit the ballyhoo we'd tied onto double-sized hooks. Tim and Charlie each fished a rod, and the girls switched off on a third one. That put one line too many in the water and it was a job keeping them untangled, particularly when we got into a school of small fish who kept hooking themselves on baits that were only slightly smaller than they were.

Cap Landau saw the sailfish's dorsal fin before any of the rest of us. He touched Judy's shoulder. She was manning the center rod.

"Lady, dere he was," he said. "Do la'k I say."

"Where?" yelled Charlie. "What?"

He started to reel in. Landau stopped him with a wave of his hand.

I stared back to where Judy's bait was skipping along on top of the deep blue water. There was a flurry of motion, a cascade of white froth.

"Let go de drag," Landau said. "Let him take de bait."

Judy released the drag lever. Line spooled out. His hand tightened on her shoulder. "Now," he said. "Set de drag." She did. He counted three silently, then shouted, "Hit dat fish!"

She pumped the rod twice. It bent sharply, and the tightened drag whined as line spooled out. Her shoulders bent under the struggle.

Good old Charlie set his own rod in a holder and started to move over to her. "I'll help," he said.

Cap pushed him back. "Don' touch dat rod," he growled. "Let her work her own fish, dass ra't. Everybody, reel in."

Tim and Charlie hauled in their lines. Judy bent herself to the slow job of raising the sailfish. Under the hot sun, it was brutal work. She'd gain fifty yards of line, and then the fish would take back a hundred. But after ten minutes he started to jump and tailwalk, and Cap beamed a wide smile.

"Now, you got 'im," he said. "He done full up wid air. Jus' keep pumpin' dat rod."

Once, when she slipped and was almost pulled from the chair, Charlie reached out a helping hand. Landau shoved him so hard that he almost went over the side.

"Nobody touch nuthin'," Landau ordered. "Dat may be a record fish. I ain't never seen one in dis close."

He handed me a pair of heavy cotton gloves. "Grab 'im by de bill when I gaff dat big boy," he said.

Slowly, inch by inch, the white monofilament line was wound onto Judy's reel, and then the steel leader came into view.

"Kotch dat leader!" Cap ordered. I got hold of it and started pulling it in. Cap stood ready with the sharply hooked gaff pole. Charlie pushed in close, a Kodak Instamatic pressed to his eye.

When I grabbed the sailfish's bill in my right hand, he gave a lurch and the boat heeled. Charlie started to go over the side. I caught his belt with my left hand. He kept slipping, and now the sailfish was almost free of my grasp.

"I can't hang onto both of them!" I yelled.

"Save the fish!" Judy shrieked.

"You're the boss," I said.

I let go of Charlie's belt and got both hands around the fish's sandpaper-covered bill. Charlie let out a whooping yell and fell overboard with a huge splash.

Cap gaffed the sailfish and we hauled it, flopping and spraying salt water, into the cockpit. It was the biggest damned fish I'd ever seen. It was longer than I was tall.

Tim helped Charlie, spluttering and sneezing, into the boat.

He staggered to his feet and threw a clumsy punch at me. I ducked under it.

"You did that on purpose!" he accused.

"It was you or the fish," I said.

Judy pulled him away. "You're not made of sugar," she said. "Oh, isn't he beautiful?"

The fish was, but the beauty was vanishing. As he died, the iridescent colors—blue and green and gold— flickered and faded to a dull silver gray.

Cap had a cloth tape measure out and was stringing it along the sailfish's back. He stood up.

"Dat one damn big fish, I ga-ron-TEE!" he said. "Jus' two inch from de record."

Charlie brightened. "Hey," he said, "I read about a muscle you can cut in the neck. That'll add four, five inches and—"

Disgusted, Cap turned away. Judy said, "Oh, no. Anyway, who cares about records?"

I gave her a beer. Her eyes met mine, and I smiled at her.

"You should be proud," I said.

"Are you going to have him mounted?" Tim asked. Judy hesitated. "Should I?"

"Yes ma'am," said Cap Landau. "You do dat t'ing."

It never occurred to me, on the way in, that by radioing ahead about our catch, Cap Landau was putting me in danger. I didn't even notice the cameraman, at first, as we hauled the fish from beneath the canvas protecting it from the sun and strung it up with the winch on the dock.

I was stretching out the sail to make a better photo for Judy when I realized that it wasn't a souvenir photographer out there. I jumped back, but not before his shutter had clicked.

"Hey, I didn't catch it," I said. "The lady did." I shoved her toward the fish.

"Smile," said the photographer. "This will probably be in the *Times-Picayune.*" He squeezed off four or five exposures.

When he was through, I moved over close and asked quietly, "You're not going to put my picture in the paper, are you?"

"Probably not," he said. "You're just the mate, aren't you?"

"That's all," I said. "Nobody'd be interested in me."

"New in town?"

"Why?"

136

"You talk funny."

"Yeah," I said. "I'm a Northerner. From At—from Pennsylvania."

He studied me. "No, you don't talk like a Yankee."

His scrutiny bothered me. "Look," I said, "can I have that picture you took of me?"

"You mean you want to buy a print?"

"I mean the negative."

"No way," he said, moving away. "This film is *Times-Picayune* property. I couldn't give it to you if I wanted to."

While he was interviewing Judy, he put his camera down. It was a Nikon 35mm with a black case.

Cap must have seen what I did. He stepped over into the shadows with me.

"What you got against picture taking?" he asked.

I grinned at him. "I don't know what you're talking about."

When the photographer bent down to pick up his camera, he found its back open and the film light-struck. He tore the yellow strip out of the camera, cursing, and threw it in the water.

"Don't be a litterbug," I said.

Reloading, he muttered, "Smart-ass." Then he took some more pictures of Judy standing near the fish and left without speaking to me again.

While the men from the taxidermy company were taking down the sailfish, I asked Judy, "How about a

137

cold martini to celebrate?"

Charlie said heavily, "Betty and Tim are waiting, Judy. We used my car, remember."

"That's right," she said. She hesitated, then added, "You drive them to the motel, Charlie. I'll get a cab home later."

He moved toward us. "I want you to come along. Right now."

His voice was ugly. It made me bristle. I looked at Judy.

"How about that, Judy?" I asked. "Do you want to go along right now?"

Deliberately, she stared at him and said, "No, I think I'd rather stay and have that martini."

Charlie's mouth opened and closed just like the sailfish's had. "But—"

I thought of a dozen wisecracks, but didn't say any of them.

Charlie couldn't even think of one. He left, practically stamping his foot.

Cap Landau gave me a broad wink. "My day to clean up dat boat," he said. "See you in de mornin'."

"Right," I said.

As I led Judy up to the parking lot, she said, "You weren't very nice to poor Charlie."

"You weren't very nice to poor Charlie either."

"That's because I don't really like poor Charlie very much," she said, laughing.

138

"Then why did you go fishing with him?"

"Because none of the fellows I meet at work ever asked me."

"I didn't think you remembered me," I said.

"Who do you think booked the *Marie II*?"

"Clever lady."

We got into the car.

"Still," she said, "it's a disappointment to learn that your boy friend isn't willing to fight for you."

"Don't be too hard on him," I said. "Charlie's a good example of the Doctor Spock generation. He was raised in a world where conflict was forbidden—whatever Charlie wanted, Charlie got, just by crying for it. He doesn't know what it's like to lose, so he doesn't know how to fight for anything."

"My, my," she said, fluffing up her tangled hair. "A profound fisherman."

"I used to be a profound vending machine technician," I said.

"Don't remind me," she said. "Hoss wanted to murder you. What went wrong, Kirby?"

"I don't know," I said honestly. "I just couldn't concentrate."

"And fishing is better?"

"Yes, I think it is. There's something about the water."

There was a pause. She asked, "Where's that martini you mentioned?"

"It could be at my place."

She laughed. "Oh, no. Too fast, my friend. Way too fast."

I turned the key. "Then that leaves Sloppy Joe's."

The bar was crowded with sports fishermen, shrimpers, tourists and college kids. It was phony Hemingway, right down to the name stolen from Key West. But the martinis were icy-cold and came in glasses as big as fish bowls.

Looking at hers, Judy said, "I think my limit is one."

"A wise decision," I said. I toasted. "To your almost record sailfish."

"Thanks," she said. "But Charlie nearly ruined everything."

"It wasn't really his fault," I said, feeling charitable. "He just got overeager."

"Yes," she said, a touch of bitterness in her voice. "That's the story of our relationship."

"Sorry," I said. "How long you been working for Hoss?"

"Two months. Before that I was a window decorator."

"And before that?"

"A lot of things." She didn't go on.

We drank. After a while, I asked, "How about dinner tonight?"

She shook her head.

"Okay," I said, figuring it was the brush.

She touched my hand. "Tomorrow?"

"Sure. But why not tonight?"

"Tonight I'll be telling Charlie where to move his toothbrush."

Zap. Just like that. The new morality. I managed a grin. "Not on my account, I hope. Like the lady said, too fast."

She gave me a wan smile. "No, it's not you. Not really. It's just that today was only one more in a long list of bad days. He knows it's coming. He's known all along. Maybe that's part of what's wrong with him."

Suddenly I felt sorry for poor Charlie. I tried to put it out of my mind. She said something.

"What?" I asked.

"I said, why did you do it?"

"Do what?"

"Ruin that photographer's film."

"Ruin—"

"Don't lie. I *saw* you, Kirby."

The room seemed to turn cold. I looked at her and wondered who I was really looking at.

"It's getting late," I said, checking my watch.

I stood, so she had to get up, too. But she didn't move toward the door.

"Off limits, huh?" she said in a small voice.

"I really better help Cap clean up the *Marie*," I said. "Let me put you in that cab you mentioned."

Anger flared in her eyes. "Don't bother!" she said, running toward the door.

I found the pay phone and dialed Noodle's private number.

When he answered, I said, "Noodle? Listen, I want you to check somebody out for me."

FIVE

I FELT bad about the way I had treated Judy, and a little silly at having turned the Justice Department loose on her. I intended to call the next morning, as soon as I'd finished hosing down the boat, which despite his generous offer the past night, Cap hadn't done. But she beat me to it. I was still swabbing the deck when she turned up on the pier.

Mopping my dripping forehead, I looked up and saw her. I put down the mop.

"Anything I can do for you?"

She said, unconcerned, "I thought I'd check on my fish. Did it go off to the taxidermist?"

"In an armored car," I said.

She reddened. "I didn't think you'd stolen it! I just—"

I climbed up on the dock. "I'll get your receipt."

She stopped me. "Look—I'm sorry. Okay?"

I said, "Sorry for what?"

"Don't play games with me, friend!" she said. "We were getting along fine last night and then I asked a question that got too close to some secret hiding place of yours, and all of a sudden it was 'See you around' time. Frankly, Kirby, that wasn't exactly what I had in mind."

I gave her Paul Newman-Number 3. "Apology accepted," I said.

She gave me a little slap. "Who else is apologizing?"

"Me," I said.

Walking her up the dock toward the parking lot, I held her hand. It was nice to feel small fingers squeezing within my own again.

"I still don't know what I said wrong," she told me.

"Don't push it," I said.

She gave me an appraising look, accepted what I'd said. "Okay," she said.

I stopped near a bank of vending machines.

"Want a Coke?"

"Love it," she said with a curious lilt to the word love. It made kind of a squeak.

The machine accepted my quarter, belched, but didn't give me a Coke.

"Okay, you son of a bitch," I said. "You're asking for it."

I hit the coin return, got back my quarter, and then gave the machine a shot with the heel of my hand just to the left of center, where the trigger mechanism was located.

Two Cokes came out, one right after the other. I jolted the machine again to shut it off.

144

"Oh, wow," said Judy. "If Hoss ever saw you doing that—"

"I only do it when the machine tries to cheat me," I said. I peered at the machines. "Do these belong to Hoss?"

She checked the name plate. "No, I was wrong. These are from Central Vending. Go ahead, hit it some more. The enemy."

"Maybe I feel the same way about machines from Gaskins, Inc."

"Bite my tongue," Judy said. "Well, what *can* we talk about? The weather?"

We leaned on the rail and watched the water.

Sipping the Coke, I asked, "Where are you from?"

"Good old Middle America. And like all girls from Nebraska, I wanted to be Doris Day."

"Are you a singer?"

She nodded. "As in 'lousy.' We had a little combo, played third-rate clubs for the beer crowd. Some talent agent booked us on what he laughingly referred to as a 'road tour.' We toured as far as Gulfport—over in Mississippi. Swell audiences. Middle-aged tourists, soldiers from Keesler Air Base. We bombed out, my friend. And when you have bombed out in Gulfport, Mississippi, there really isn't any place left to go. So the other kids went back to Chicago to try again. But I'd had enough. I came over here. I worked at a department store for a while, pinning curtains up in window displays."

"And then Hoss Gaskins gave you a chance to get away from all that."

She laughed. "The pay was better, and I didn't have to be on my feet. End of sad story. Add that the lady is twenty-six, almost married a couple of times—except at the last minute she pulled back because it always seemed so silly. I mean, what was I signing up for? I'm one of your modern females, sir, so there wasn't any big mystery about the bed side of it. What else was there? Three kids, bang, bang, bang, one right after the other, and then into the role of part-time chauffeur—driving Dad to the office and the kids to school—and then, hi-de-ho, off for the big thrill of the supermarket? Yechh."

"Bitter, bitter," I said.

She whirled on me. "You bet I'm bitter, friend. Look, Kirby—I'm no women's libber. I just like to feel I have some small say over what I'm going to do with this life of mine. Except I keep picking up pages of script that have me talking like Little Mary Sunshine."

I put our empty bottles back in the rack. "If you expect me to play into that one, you're humming the wrong tune, baby."

She studied me. "You know, friend, we can flirt around the bush all day long, but sooner or later you're going to tell me."

"Tell you what?"

"What it is you're hiding from."

*　*　*

I had a date with her at seven. But first I met Noodle at five in a waterfront bar. We sat in the corner and had a beer.

Consulting his notes, he said, "Judy Taylor. Twenty-six. Born, Lincoln, Nebraska. Attended Northwestern University, Chicago. Didn't complete her final year. Only one bust on her record—when Chicago narcs raided a pot party. She wasn't holding, got off with a suspended sentence. She sang in three or four North Side night clubs, nothing big, then went on the road with a small group. They folded in Mississippi."

"Is she hooked up with the syndicate?"

"No, but she knows people who are." He hesitated. "However, that's normal, if you're working in Chicago. There's syndicate money in most of the clubs there."

I stared down into my glass. "So they could have sent her out to spot me."

"How, Kirby? She's been here in New Orleans more than a year. Until a few months ago, the syndicate didn't know you existed. And nobody but me even knows you're in Louisiana." He drained his beer. "Forget it. Let me do the worrying. If you start seeing gangsters in every shadow, you'll twist your neck off looking over your own shoulder."

"So Judy's okay?"

"As far as we're concerned. Whether she's okay for you is something between the two of you."

I started to get up. "Thanks, Noodle."

He waved me back into the chair.

"Hold it. I've got some more good news for you."

I felt a tingle of anticipation. "Brian's letter."

"No. But Cade's called off his troops on the street back in Atlanta. Nobody's looking for you any more."

Slowly, I asked, "What does that mean?"

"We'll play it safe for a while, but there's a very good chance that the contract on you has been canceled. Cade's partners never were in favor of it from the beginning."

Dryly, I said, "Dissension among thieves. Wouldn't that be great."

"Come on, Kirby," said Noodle, waving for two more beers. "Have one on me. Things are getting better. I can *feel* it."

The clerk in the Georgia Motor Vehicle Bureau told the patrolman, "I'm sorry, officer. I've run all the combinations of name and initials. We don't have a current address for your William Kirby. The computer shows that his license was turned in, and he hasn't applied for one in any other state."

The trooper nodded. "Well, it was just a chance," he said. "Thank you just the same, ma'am."

When he turned toward the door, anyone who knew him would have recognized Luke Martin in the brown uniform.

*　　*　　*

We had dinner at the Andrew Jackson on Royal Street.

Judy glowed in the candlelight.

"You're very pretty tonight," I told her.

She laughed. "Flattery will get you everywhere with me, my friend."

I poured wine for both of us. "Oh, I went over to the taxidermist this afternoon. They're putting a rush on your fish. And I've got a surprise."

She tilted her head. "It was discovered that all I caught was a plastic imitation."

"Nope. There's no charge for the work. They're going to give you a freebie for all the publicity involved."

She blew me a kiss. "I bet I can name who set *that* up."

"Modesty forbids," I said.

"That's right," she said with double meaning. "I'd forgotten how retiring you are."

I gave her a sharp glance and she clapped a hand over her mouth. "Whoops!" she said. "About face. Wonderful weather we're—"

"Nut," I said. "How's the wine?"

With that cute squeak in her voice, she said, "Love it."

Over coffee, I asked, "When are you coming out on the boat again?"

"When I can scare up enough wealthy tourists to

spring the hundred bucks for charter," she said.

"Friends of the First Mate ride free," I suggested.

She squeezed my hand. "You've got yourself a deal."

After dinner, we went over to Pete Fountain's to hear some jazz.

Pete wasn't there that night, but the band was in fine form. We had a slow drink and listened.

"I guess you like music," I said.

She tilted her head, opened her mouth, and before she could say it, I did: "Love it."

She bit her lower lip. "Dear me, I guess I do say that a lot, don't I?"

"That you do."

"Well, I can't help it."

"I like it."

"You do?"

"Love it," I said.

Defensively, she said, "Don't make fun of me. And I *do* love music. That's what makes me so miserable. I can hear a beautiful voice singing inside my head. My friend, I am better than Peggy Lee, Anna Maria Alberghetti and Doris Day all in one . . . until I open my mouth. Then out comes something that sounds like those noises you hear from Barbie dolls."

I leaned over and tickled her side. "Where do you pull the string?"

She slapped my hand. "Don't squeeze the merchandise."

"Sorry," I said, drawing back.

150

She held my hand. "No, it's . . . well, I just like to do all my own unwrapping."

As I pulled up near the curb, she said, "This isn't my place."

"I know," I said. "It's mine."

She studied me. "Just like that?"

I met her eyes. "Just like that."

She sighed. I reached for the key to start the engine again. Then, her voice low, she said, "Why not?"

She made me turn around before she'd undress.

"Don't look," she warned.

"Modesty?" I said with my best leer.

"Embarrassment," she said. "You've been sold a bill of goods, my friend. You've been taken in by the packaging."

I turned around. She had wrapped herself up in my bathrobe.

"Judy, what the hell are you talking about?"

"This," she said, tossing her black bra to me. I caught it. It seemed to weigh a pound. It was heavily padded.

"How about that," I said. "They come off."

"All those lovely curves and uplift were courtesy of Maidenform," she said. She picked up the drink I'd made when we came in.

"But why?"

Bitterly, she said, "So I could stick out up there like all those goddamned healthy bayou girls with their

151

lousy thirty-eight double C cups, why the hell do you think?"

I reached for her. "I don't know why, babe, but I think you're trying to turn me off."

Hesitantly, she said, ". . . Maybe I am."

"Why?"

She snuggled in my arms. "Because I'm afraid."

"Don't be," I said, reaching for the light switch.

I've never been inside a Credit Bureau office. Apparently Luke Martin knew his way around them very well. He waited patiently while the manager of one in Atlanta examined read-outs coming from a computer.

The manager was saying, "We're always glad to cooperate with you folks from Internal Revenue."

"We appreciate it," said the Bookkeeper.

"Now, if this William Kirby of yours has so much as signed a gas station bill on credit, he'll be in our computer banks. International Credit is the biggest in the business. We have offices in every state."

"We know," said the Bookkeeper. "That's why I came to you."

The manager laughed. "Of course," he said, "I somehow had the idea *your* outfit was even bigger."

"We try to work with private firms as much as possible," said the Bookkeeper. "It's more democratic."

The manager of Atlanta's International Credit Bureau tore off the read-out, examined it carefully, and said, "Now, how about that?"

"Finished?"

"Sorry, Mr. Boyd," said the manager. "This Kirby fellow—"

"What?"

"Looks like he closed out every credit card and charge account he ever had. Paid cash on the line. He doesn't have a cent on the books."

"Does that mean you can't trace him?"

The manager forced a laugh. "I wish we could. Right now, he's got a Triple A credit rating."

Sometime during the night, I woke up and sat near the window. The street light flooded in under the shade, illuminating Judy's sleeping face on my extra pillow.

It made me feel good. She seemed to belong there.

The aching loneliness had eased a little.

Of course, it's never perfect. But maybe you already know that.

Next morning I was working on my charts. I had set myself the job of trying to memorize the channels into the lake from the Gulf. The chart was covered with neat, lightly penciled trackings.

Judy was making a big fuss out of straightening the apartment. Maybe she thought she was. To me it was obvious that she was checking everything out.

She poured me some more coffee.

"Thanks," I said.

"Want some sugar?"

Trying to concentrate on the chart, I said, "Nope."

"How about some toast?"

"Judy, will you find someplace and light?"

"I'm bored," she said.

"Just let me get this one approach nailed down, and—"

"Oh, all right," she said tightly. "If you only kept this place as neat as you do those charts—"

I shut off her voice inside my head. But it didn't work for long.

"You really ought to get a maid to come in a couple of times a week."

I made a line on the chart, saw it was in the wrong place, and started to erase it.

She opened the hall closet and grimaced at the pile of dirty clothes there.

"And when was the last time you took out your laundry?"

I didn't answer. She flipped through the clothing hanging from the rack.

"You've got three nice sports jackets in here," she called. "How come you only wear that striped one?"

I bent over the chart and tried to ignore her. From the corner of my eye I saw her checking out the top shelf. Too late, I remembered what was there. She picked it up.

Holding the framed photograph, she said, "Hey, who's this?"

I didn't answer. She came over to me, carrying it. "Kirby, who's this little boy?"

Without raising my voice, I said, trembling, "Judy, put it back where you found it."

She didn't hear the anger. Unknowing, she went on: "Why are you hiding a picture of a little boy in your hall closet?"

I almost slapped her and then converted the move into a wild, pointing gesture. "Damn it, I said *put it back!*"

I saw the hurt spring to her eyes. She replaced the picture on the shelf, closed the door. I stared at her.

"I'm sorry," she murmured.

"Forget it," I said. I meant it to mean just what it said, but even to my own ears my voice was angry and mean.

"I think I'd better go," she said.

I tried to salvage something. "Judy, it's only—"

She broke. "Oh, *shove* it!" she screamed, and ran out.

I got up and went to the door. It was half open. I heard her running down the stairs.

I could have gone after her. But I didn't.

I closed the door and went to the closet.

She had left Brian's picture upright. He smiled his eight-year-old, gap-toothed grin at me.

I laid him down flat on the shelf and closed the closet door.

To anyone who knew him, Luke Martin would have looked odd in his ten-gallon hat, cowboy boots, and slash-pocket, fringed jacket. But to the Atlanta bank vice president he was Texas Money, and the banker said sir often.

Consulting a file, the banker said, "Yes, that mortgage is still in effect. No delinquencies. Sir."

"Does Mr. Kirby pay it directly?" asked the Bookkeeper.

"He used to, but recently a local attorney has been handling the account."

"What's his name?"

"Mr. Harvey Baker. Sir. Right here in Atlanta."

The Bookkeeper nodded, hiding his disappointment.

Anxiously, the banker said, "They might want to sell, Mr. Corby. Naturally, the bank will be happy to cooperate in every way, particularly since this parcel is only a small part of the total holding you want to acquire. But I'm afraid you'll have to work through Mr. Baker. Much as I'd like to enter the picture, you must recognize our conflict of interest—"

"Thanks," said the Bookkeeper. "I'll let you know."

When Luke Martin had gone, the banker hesitated. He frowned. Had he gone too far?

He decided to copper his bet.

He picked up the phone.

"Sally, get me a local attorney named Harvey Baker. No, I don't know his number. I'll hold."

Judy was waiting for me when the *Marie II* came in. She didn't say anything, and neither did I. We walked to my car and got in.

I didn't start the engine.

"You've got a right to know," I said. "That was my son."

She touched my cheek. "I was being nosy. I'm sorry."

"I've been married," I said, rushing the words. "Now I'm divorced and they live in another city."

"You don't have to tell me," she said.

"That's all," I said. I had stopped myself barely in time to keep from letting her know the whole god-damned mess. My voice shook as I asked, "How about a martini?"

Her voice shook, too. "Love it," she said.

SIX

THE Bookkeeper was clever, but gradually his investigations began to make tiny waves—waves that spread until they reached the ears of the Justice Department.

Baker requested a tie line to Noodle. Of course, he still didn't know who Noodle was, or in what city he worked.

The connection was bad. Naturally.

"I said," Baker repeated, "we've got indications that a professional's on Kirby's trail. How have things been going there?"

"We had a little trouble at first," Noodle said. "Adjustment shock, the handbook calls it."

"And now?"

"He seems to be doing better. He's got a girl friend."

"Is that such a good idea? So soon?"

"Mr. Baker, it's his life to live."

"Noodle, I want to see him."

158

"Why?"

"I've got an itch. Something's not kosher. Maybe Kirby's one of those who can never go underground successfully. Let's get together in a neutral city."

"I wouldn't want to tell you your business, Mr. Baker, but is that wise?"

"Nobody will follow me, I'll make sure of that. I'll use a Department Jetstar."

"No, I meant that the whole purpose of this relocation was to sever all ties Kirby had with his past. Won't you just be opening those old wounds up again?"

"I can't help it," Baker said. "Where do you suggest?"

There was a pause. "How about Montgomery, Alabama?"

"Fine," said Baker. "I'll make arrangements with airport security to use their VIP suite."

"How do you know they've got one?"

Baker laughed. "Noodle, every airport in the world has one, just in case Raquel Welch ever passes through."

By the time Baker's message was relayed to me, I was already in trouble again.

Judy and I were walking in Jackson Square after dinner. It was a mild night for December.

"It's beautiful," Judy said.

Tightly, I said, "Keep walking."

"What?"

"I think somebody's following us."

She gave a nervous laugh. "Oh, Kirby! Following us? Why?"

We turned a corner. I yanked her back into the shadows. When the man behind us came around the corner, I grabbed him by one wrist and pulled him into the darkness. He hit the side of the building with a solid thud.

"Okay, buddy!" I said. "What do you want?"

"Huh?" said the man. He was bigger than me, but drunker too, which made it even.

"Why the hell are you following us?"

"Maybe the lady gave me the eye," he said, a touch of Cajun accent in his voice.

Furious, I slugged him. It almost broke my hand. His jaw was made of concrete. He rubbed it. He hadn't even seemed to feel the blow.

Slowly, he said, "Boy, I'm going to tear you apart."

Judy said, "Stop it, both of you!"

He started toward me. "You don't hit Old Tim like that and walk home, Coon-ass."

I hit him again, this time in the gut. He coughed a little, but still gathered me up in his arms and began to squeeze me like a big bear. I jammed my heel down on the arch of his foot and he released me, letting out a whooping yell.

A crowd gathered from nowhere. I hit him again and he backed up against the building.

"Boy, you're getting me mad," he said.

160

"Kirby!" Judy said. "Stop it!"

By then it was too late. Two policemen had arrived.

The tall one said, "Okay, what's the trouble here?"

The big man seemed to sober instantly. "Just a friendly fight among buddies," he said clearly, obviously afraid of the cops. "Nothing to get excited about."

The policemen seemed to relax. The ready hands moved away from revolver butts.

Then I fouled it up. "This bastard's no friend of mine," I said. "He was following us." I knew I was wrong, but I couldn't shut off my mouth.

The shorter policeman studied me. "Now why would he do something like that?" he drawled.

Realizing that I'd called attention to myself, I tried to get out of it. "I don't know. Maybe he wasn't. I must have made a mistake."

The tall one said, "What's your name?"

"Bill Kirby," I said. I clapped my mouth shut, aghast. But it was too late.

"Let's see some I.D."

I hauled it out. The tall policeman flipped through my wallet, frowning.

Judy, her voice shrill, said, "William Kirby Grant, you've gone and done it now. I told you that Tim was only an old friend, but you had to get jealous and—"

"Hold it down, lady," said the shorter policeman as his buddy peered through my identification.

Increasing the shrillness, Judy plowed on: "—And it was going to be such a nice evening, too. I—"

161

"Lady, please," said the tall one. To me: "Is that your whole name? William Kirby Grant?"

Weakly, I said, "Yes."

"I don't see no William on these. They all read 'Kirby Grant,' and that's all."

Judy shrilled, "He *hates* his given name, William. Did you ever hear such a silly thing?" She whirled on me. "Why is *that*, William Kirby Grant? Just because your father was named William too and you never got along with him—"

The tall policeman said, "Ma'am, we'd sure appreciate it if you wouldn't talk so much."

"Well!" she said, stamping her foot. "And here I thought you two were such nice officers, keeping the peace—"

Both of them had had more than enough of her. The tall one gave me back my wallet, shaking his head. "Okay," he said. "But I want to warn both you boys, no more fighting in the streets. You understand?"

The big man said, nodding, "You've got my word on that, Sherf."

I nodded, too. I couldn't talk. I stared at Judy, amazed at her quick presence of mind.

The policemen pointed the big man back toward Jackson Square. Judy and I started up the narrow street toward Bourbon.

"Judy," I began, "I—"

Grimly, she said, "You've got some serious explaining to do, Mr. William Kirby."

*   *   *

"I thought I'd blown the whole deal for sure," I told Noodle. "Then Judy jumped in and bailed me out. My God, what if they'd hauled me in and taken my fingerprints?"

"The FBI would have reported back that you're Kirby Grant with no previous arrests. Kirby, stop sweating it. There's not a record anywhere in the world identifying you with your past."

"Nowhere but in here," I said, tapping my forehead.

"That's where the trouble is," he agreed. "So you've told Judy the truth?"

"No," I said, staring out the jet's window at the Alabama countryside below. We'd just taken off from a stop at Mobile. I wondered if Nancy with the laughing face was driving one of those cars down there.

"Take my advice," Noodle said. "Don't."

"You cleared her yourself."

"It's still not worth the risk," he said.

"Well, I've got to tell her something," I said. "She's been awful good about it, but she's not going to sit still for much more mystery man stuff."

"Kirby, take my word, nobody can find you in New Orleans. Nobody can blow the whistle on you—nobody but you yourself. Don't make a big mistake."

"And you guys never make mistakes?" I laughed. "How about that witness you relocated in San Francisco? Some bonehead in Justice issued him, and his wife, *and* his mother-in-law Social Security cards with

163

consecutive numbers. It took the mob exactly three weeks to track him down. Do you call that smart?"

"Nobody's perfect," Noodle said. I didn't react. "That was supposed to be a joke," he added.

"Ha, ha," I said.

The blinds were drawn in the VIP suite. Baker was waiting. Noodle shook hands with him.

"Thanks," said Baker. "I'll send for you when we're through."

"I think I'll have a beer," Noodle said.

"Drink one for me," I told him. "No hard feelings."

When we were alone, I turned to Baker. "Why the hell hasn't my boy been writing?"

"They've been away," he said.

"Are you sure about that? There's no trouble?"

"Your mother-in-law was sick. She's getting better."

"I want to talk with my son."

"Kirby," Baker said, "this is the first time I've ever broken the departmental rules about contacting a witness who has gone underground."

I looked at my bruised knuckles. "I guess I've been fouling up, huh?"

"That's an understatement," he said. "You don't like it very much, do you?"

"Hell no. Would you?"

"I suppose not. Kirby, what can I do to help?"

"Easy," I said. "You can put me back together again, in my own town, with my own name and my own son."

"I wish we could," he said.

Sarcastically, I mimicked, " 'Be a good citizen,' you said. 'Testify against the nasty gangster, and don't worry, we'll take care of you.' Well, you took care of me all right. I'm nothing now. I'm just a patchwork man, made up of bits and pieces stolen from somebody else's past. I'm stuck together with spit and glue. No wonder the first strong wind that comes along blows me to pieces. What the hell kind of life is that?"

"It's better than no life at all. Kirby, they've brought in one of their big guns. A professional hit man. I don't think there's any way he can trace you to your relocation, but maybe we shouldn't take the chance."

"I'm already buried ten feet deep. What else can you do to me?"

"We can put you under protective custody."

"You mean, hide me out in some jail?"

"It would be safer."

"For how long?"

He spread his hands. That was no answer.

"You don't know, do you? Is it a year?" He didn't respond. "Five? The rest of my life?"

"This ought to blow over soon. When we heard Cade had called off the local troops, we thought it was finished then. But they can't afford to hunt for you forever."

"Christ!" I said. "How the hell did I ever get into this? How did I let you bastards sucker me into testifying?"

"It's still a good thing that you did, Kirby."

165

"Sure," I said, furiously angry. "All right, my friend, now you listen to me. Forget about protective custody. You're lucky I'm even going back to N—back to where I am. And I'm telling you now, I'm seeing my kid for Christmas. Have you got those two facts straight, Mr. Baker?" He nodded. "And one more thing. When you get back to Atlanta, you call up that bitch ex-wife of mine and tell her I want a letter from my boy. Right *now!*"

"I'll do my best," he said. "Don't be too disturbed, Kirby. When their pro doesn't turn you up, they'll get smart and call the whole thing off."

"When?"

"Pretty soon."

"How long is 'pretty soon'?"

"Maybe a year," he said.

Baker kept his word. When he got back to Atlanta, he called Lucille.

"Yes, Mr. Baker," she said. "I'm sorry. We've been away." She hesitated. "But I'll make sure Brian writes. I suppose we owe Bill that much."

She hung up.

If she'd looked out the window with night glasses, she might have seen a small panel truck parked across the street. Luke Martin was in back with a cassette tape recorder hooked into a portable FM radio receiver. He switched off the tape, crawled up front into the driver's seat, and drove away.

He had two adjoining rooms in a nearby motel. He sat at a table in the larger room. His finger pressed the "Play" button on the recorder.

A youngish, blonde woman leaned forward and listened.

Lucille's voice said, "I'm sorry. We've been away. But I'll make sure Brian writes. I suppose we owe Bill that much."

"Stella?" said the Bookkeeper.

Concentrating, the young woman said—in a voice that was an almost perfect imitation of Lucille's—"I'll make sure Brian writes. I suppose we owe Bill that much."

"Good," he said. "But you can do better. Keep working on it."

The Christmas decorations seem to come earlier every year. Sometimes I suspect they don't even take them down any more.

But they're cheerful, unless you're lonely, in which case they can be painful.

This Christmas was sort of in between. I wasn't dancing any jigs, but Judy's presence helped some.

We walked along Canal Street, looking in the windows. How long had it been since Lucille and I had window-shopped? Forever, I guess. That's the kind of thing you do before you're married, when you want to be together and there's no place to go.

"Twelve more shopping days," Judy said.

167

"Are you going home?"

"To *Nebraska?* Are you kidding? I came down here to get away from snow, remember?"

We walked awhile. Then she asked, "What about you?"

"I don't know," I said. "I think I may go to Atlanta."

"Atlanta? Gee-ay? Why not Jamaica or Puerto Rico? Now, friend, if you were going to Puerto Rico, I wouldn't be at all surprised if you couldn't find a certain crow-voiced ex-singer who'd be delighted to pay her own air fare—"

We meandered down along the Mississippi. "Honey," I said, "let's find somewhere to sit down."

"Good idea," she said.

We found a phony Gay Nineties bar, complete with blacked-up minstrel singers and mustached bartenders. We took a table near the bandstand, where a buxom blonde sat on a red velvet swing belting out "Shine On, Harvest Moon."

I nodded toward the false gaiety. "Too bad it wasn't *really* like this."

"I wish I could understand you," she said. "Why are you so unhappy? Why are you so bitter?"

"I guess I'm just a bitter guy," I said.

"No, you're not. Oh, I realize that you've never let me see the real you. But sometimes you relax and it almost comes through, and then I can guess what you must truly be like. But, my friend, those moments are

168

rare. Mostly, it's like watching you reflected in a mirror that fell down and cracked—"

"And somebody patched up, but not too well?"

"Something like that."

Our beer came in tall, foaming mugs. I gulped at mine and made my decision.

"Well, why not?" I said. "It's true. I *am* all patched up. Judy, I'm not who you think I am. My real name *is* Bill Kirby."

Without a smile, she said, "I guessed *that* the other night."

"Well, here's something you didn't guess," I said.

I told her.

My words droned on, only half audible even to my own ears. If you had been nearby, the male quartet which had appeared to render "While Strolling Through the Park One Day" would have given a false cheerfulness to the setting, and you probably wouldn't have heard more than an occasional word. ". . . Syndicate." ". . . Justice Department." ". . . I was taken by surprise by a pair of roguish eyes—" But, no, that's part of the song, isn't it?

Before I'd finished, tears were rolling down her cheeks.

Unbelievingly, Judy said, "And they took *everything* away from you? Your business, your home, your name —even your son?"

I nodded. She stared down at the rings her beer mug

169

had made on the table.

"My God! I didn't think things like that really happened."

"They really happen," I said.

"For how long?"

"It could be for the rest of my life," I said.

"Oh, how awful," she said, stroking my hand. Two black-faced banjo players came up next to us and began strumming away at "Yes Sir, That's My Baby."

"Kirby—Bill—"

"Yes, Judy?"

"Let's go home."

That was the night the Bookkeeper invaded my house on Peachtree View.

He'd paid off a friendly telephone repairman to install the FM bug in the terminal box where the line entered the house. But now that he wanted something from the interior itself, Luke Martin would not trust it to anyone but himself.

Without knowing it was a regular escape route for Brian and me, he chose the back side of the house where the tree branch led to Brian's room.

He wore heavy goggles and carried a special flashlight that threw a beam visible only through their infrared lenses.

Brian was sleeping. I don't know what the Bookkeeper would have done if he'd awakened. His pockets were filled with equipment. Perhaps he would only have smothered Brian into unconsciousness with a drug-soaked cloth. Perhaps he would have done worse.

He found what he was looking for—a thin packet of letters from me. With them snuggled in his pocket, he crept out again without a sound.

Gus would never had allowed this intrusion.

But, of course, Lucille had never liked Gus.

The letters were spread out on the motel table.

Stella, the blonde girl, studied them.

"They've been readdressed," she said. "Atlanta postmarks. And he never mentions where he is. Except that it's warm."

"Make sure that door is locked," said Luke Martin, unpacking a small fingerprint kit. He treated the surface of each letter with a chemical spray.

"Fingerprints?" said Stella wonderingly. This was the first time she'd ever worked with the Bookkeeper. Her home was in Detroit, and she'd been recommended for this job by a captain in the infamous Purple Gang who had received a long-distance call from Luke Martin.

"Quiet," he said. Quickly, he applied fixative to one letter which had more than a dozen prints on its margins. I would have recognized this one. It was written shortly after I'd gotten to New Orleans, and I had struggled over it for more than an hour to keep my despondency from sneaking into its lines.

Carefully, referring to a small handbook, Luke Martin began to code the prints. From each whorl "landmark" he drew a line out to the margin and assigned it a number. When he was finished, he transcribed the various numbers into a nine-digit sequence.

"Now," he said, "let's see what police force we own."

He dialed the phone.

Tony D'Amato answered on the third ring.

"Is that you, Luke?"

"I want some fingerprints checked through Washington," said the Bookkeeper.

"I don't know," D'Amato said slowly. "Luke, there's been a change in plans—"

"Don't stall me, D'Amato," said the Bookkeeper. "You must have some tame sheriff who'll run these through FBI."

"Luke," D'Amato said anxiously, "I think the contract's off."

"Who says so?"

"The boys. They found out about it and they're really pissed."

"Has Harry Cade called it off?"

"I ain't talked to him yet," said D'Amato.

"Well, you do that little thing before you shoot off your mouth again," said the Bookkeeper. "Meanwhile, I want a name."

Miserably, D'Amato said, "Okay, Luke. See Sheriff Rembert Brown, up in Leesville."

"Brown," said the Bookkeeper. "And, D'Amato—"

"What?"

"Don't call me Luke."

SEVEN

LEESVILLE, Georgia, is just another small town in the process of being swallowed up by the urban sprawl. Until ten years or so ago, it was best known for the quality—and quantity—of the bootleg white lightning whiskey produced there under the benevolent but watchful eye of a cooperative sheriff's department.

Today, many of the old guard have been thrown out of office and moonshine liquor is a thing of the past. But some of the olden ways hang on.

It's hard to explain certain kinds of Southern law enforcement. All of the stereotypes you see in movies and on TV are right—yet they're wrong, too. Remember that red-neck sheriff in the movie, *In the Heat of the Night*? Well, I've met him a hundred times in small Southern towns, and he's just as bigoted and opinionated as Rod Steiger made him out to be. He's likely to be on the take from a dozen small-time rackets, and a delighted sparkle comes to his eye when he spots a speeding out-of-towner. He'll ask you politely—once—

to move on, or stand up, or shut up, or whatever the request may be. The second time, he uses his fists. Or billy club.

Then, when you least expect it, this corrupt, loud-mouthed, violent man will lay his life on the line to protect you or your property. If you're out of town, he'll take it on himself—often on his own time—to check out your house to be sure it's unmolested. If you have one too many, instead of heaving you into the hoosegow to sober up, he'll confiscate your car keys and drive you home himself.

You figure it out. I guess what I'm getting at is that I couldn't really get angry at Sheriff Rembert Brown for taking the Bookkeeper's crisp new fifty dollar bill and relaying his request for identification to the FBI Fingerprint Center in Washington, D.C.

Like so many law enforcement offices now, Brown had a TWX which, through phone lines, was hooked into Washington when he dialed the proper prefix and typed the correct identification code on his keyboard.

An FBI employee, a young woman, tore his request off her TWX printer, studied it, and then fed a series of numbers into a computer input.

It purred for a moment, then the IBM selectric ball began to whirl and in seconds my entire new life history was retrieved and handed to her in pica, 10-pitch typewriter face.

She sat down at the TWX keyboard and began to

relay the information to Sheriff Rembert Brown of Leesville, Georgia.

A supervisor came over. She studied what the young woman was doing. She picked up the computer read-out, touched the young woman on the shoulder.

Indicating a prefix on the read-out, the supervisor asked, "Didn't you see this Code Six?"

The young woman said hesitantly, "I—"

"End your transmission," said the supervisor.

The young woman typed a quick "Message ends" on the TWX and looked up at the supervisor with apprehension.

"Information on Code Six identifications aren't relayed to anyone without Justice Department approval," the supervisor said sternly.

Luke Martin had been watching the TWX creating its long lines of typing, untouched by human hands.

He read, "Subject fingerprints identify Kirby Grant, male, Caucasian, weight 185, height 6'1", Place of birth . . . MESSAGE ENDS MESSAGE ENDS.

"That's funny," said Sheriff Rembert Brown. "They never stopped in the middle like that before."

"That's all right," said the Bookkeeper. "His name is all I need."

Uneasily, Brown said, "I hope there ain't going to be any trouble with the FBI—"

"What trouble could there be over a routine identification request? If anybody asks you, he got picked up in a traffic violation and refused to give you his name."

"But where is he now?" Brown persisted.

"You let him go, and he never showed for trial," said the Bookkeeper. "So far as you're concerned, he dropped off the face of the earth."

The FBI sent a routine report to the Department of Justice about the request from Leesville.

Just as routinely, it was filed.

After all, nobody in Justice's central office had ever heard of any Kirby Grant.

The manager at International Credit smiled at Luke Martin. He had already fed Luke's new information into the computers, and they were waiting for the read-outs.

"You IRS men never give up, do you?" he said. "So he changed his name. What's the rap, tax evasion?"

"Routine," said the Bookkeeper. "Anyway, we're not allowed to talk about cases."

"Very sound," said the manager.

The computer began to disgorge its stored information. The manager studied the long roll of paper as it slid from the machine.

"Do you have anything on him?" asked the Book-keeper.

Examining the read-out, the manager said, "Oh, yes indeed. Several gasoline purchases. A routine credit check by Louisiana Light and Power. He's charged tabs at several restaurants. There's no doubt about it. We've found your man."

"Where?"

"All of these charges were made in New Orleans."

"Thanks," said the Bookkeeper.

"Always glad to help the government," said the manager of International Credit.

My phone rang at five A.M. It was Cap Landau.

"Kirby," he said, "I got me some trouble up in Shreveport. I got to go up dar. You take de charter today. Will you do dat?"

"Sure," I said.

I hung up and yawned. It was almost time to get up anyway. Fishing is an early-morning business.

I got dressed. Judy's perfume was still heavy in the room, but she had gone home early last night. She was expecting a call from her family.

My clients were already waiting when I got down to the dock.

"Morning," I said. "Anyone for coffee?"

"We've had ours," said one man. The group of four were from the medical convention at the Fairmont Hotel. They wore what they imagined were colorful fishing costumes. One still had a price tag on his shirt-tail. I reached over and tore it off. That blaze of red-and-blue dacron had cost him $12.95.

"Well, welcome aboard the *Marie II*," I said.

A second man, older than the other three, said, "They told us at the hotel that you know where the fish are, Cap'n Landau."

"Well, let's just say that I try harder," I said. If he wanted to think I was Landau, that was his problem.

Clumsily, they piled aboard.

The first man said, "Sorry this is only half a day. But we've got to be back at the Superdome at two."

"I hear they've got some fancy johns up on the third level," I said, trying to keep a straight face.

They laughed. They'd missed the punch line somehow, but us old Cajun fishermen are renowned for our wit.

I don't know what stopped me from pressing the red START Button. I'd turned on the bilge blowers, the vapor sniffer read "Safe." But something was wrong.

"What's the delay?" asked the older man. "We're losing time."

"I'll only be a minute," I said.

I went back and lifted the hatch.

The blowers weren't blowing. And the raw gasoline swilling around in the bilge threw up an odor that almost knocked me down.

"What's wrong?" said one of the men. He was getting ready to light his pipe.

"Don't strike that match!" I said.

"Gasoline in the bilge?" said the first man. "That's dangerous."

178

"You're telling me," I said.

I traced the power lines to the blowers and the vapor sniffer. Both were broken where they came through the bulkhead.

"What happened?" asked another man.

"If I'd touched that starter button, we'd all have been blown sky-high," I said.

My doctors didn't like that very much. They retreated to a huddle to mumble among themselves. I contemplated the gasoline floating on top of the inch or so of water in the bilge. I didn't want to start the pumps, although with the hatch open I wouldn't have to worry about an explosion.

The doctors solved my problem. The leader approached me and said, "Captain, we've been thinking. Half a day's not really long enough to do any serious fishing. Do you mind if we cancel?"

"Be my guest," I said. "I wouldn't ride on this tub today either, if it wasn't my job."

"We'll gladly pay—"

"It's on the house," I said. "Sorry about the trouble. Maybe next time."

They left. I went up to the harbormaster's shack, borrowed a plastic bilge pump, and went back to the *Marie II* and began clearing the gasoline-contaminated water out of her hull by hand.

Twenty minutes later, when I'd worked up a good sweat, two college kids in a Sailfish slid past. They glared at the rainbowed reflections the gasoline had made in the water and let go a couple of loud comments about pollution.

Cheerfully, I suggested where they could pollute themselves.

Cap wasn't too happy about the broken wires. We couldn't prove they'd been cut.

"Nothing's worth a damn any more," he said. "You shoes wear out before you take'm out of de box."

Somebody else wasn't too happy, either. Harry Cade.

Luke Martin had been keeping in touch with Tony D'Amato. Now he got a summons to appear before Cade the next day.

Martin was no dummy. Maybe he'd located me, but he wasn't about to reveal that bargaining point to Cade.

"What the hell are you doing with my money?" Cade demanded. "Having yourself a little vacation in New Orleans?"

"How did you know I was in New Orleans?" asked the Bookkeeper.

"You don't think I toss out fifty grand without keeping an eye on it, do you?"

"So you've had somebody on my trail."

"Most of the time. You shook him when you got to New Orleans."

The Bookkeeper frowned. "Did it ever occur to you that I might make the mistake of thinking your guys were working for the government?"

"So what?"

"So they still haven't found the last FBI man who tried to follow me. Call off your shadows, Cade. I won't work with you looking over my shoulder. What the hell did you get me up here for anyway? Not just to ream me out."

"No," Cade admitted. "Bookkeeper, you've got to hurry things up."

"I've found him. That's more than your whole outfit could do. What's wrong? Does the organization want to call off your contract?"

Cade hesitated. "If I were outside— Who the hell do they think I am, treating me this way? Bookkeeper, they told me I didn't have the right. The right! Who opened up this territory? They want me to cancel the hit."

"Why don't you?" Luke Martin said calmly.

"And let that fink walk around free? After he took my money and fingered me? Like hell I will. I don't care what the boys say. Listen, we've got a deal, you and me. I stand by my end. You've got to stand by yours."

"I've never failed a contract yet," said the Bookkeeper. "I'll deliver, Cade. But it may bring some heat down on you."

"I'm used to heat. But make it fast."

"I'm on his heels," said the Bookkeeper. "Do you remember Earl Schickel?"

"That rat. He dropped dead of a heart attack right in the lobby of The Sands, may he rot in hell."

"I arranged that heart attack," said the Bookkeeper. "With a new drug that no coroner in the country can detect."

"Use it again, Bookkeeper," whispered Harry Cade. "Use it."

This time, when my phone rang, Judy was there, too. She couldn't hear the message—but she could read my face.

I heard Lucille's voice.

"Bill?" she said frantically. "Bill?"

"Lucille? What's wrong?"

"Oh, Bill, you've got to come home. It's Brian. He's been hurt."

A chill closed around my heart. "What do you mean, hurt?"

"He was riding his bike on Peachtree. A car— Oh, Bill, hurry!"

"I'll be there tonight," I said.

"Come right to the house," she said.

I hung up.

The Bookkeeper had been listening on an extension. Stella said, anyway, "He'll be there."

"Good work," he told her.

He began packing his slim briefcase. Everything in it was a deadly weapon.

* * *

"But how did she know where you were?" Judy asked.

"Maybe she called Noodle." Judy stared at me blankly. "My contact here. A U.S. marshal. That's his code name."

"Call her back," she pleaded. "Make sure."

"Don't you think I know my own wife's voice?" It hurt her, but I didn't care. "Judy, I've got exactly thirty minutes to catch my plane. They need me at home."

"What about me?" she asked. "Don't I count for anything?"

"Sure you do," I said. "But—"

"But your family counts for more."

"Baby," I said, "it's my *son!*"

"And your *wife*, right, friend? You never really gave her up, not deep down, did you?"

"Judy, I don't have time to argue."

She caught my head in both her hands and pulled me to her. "I'm sorry. I know I'm being a bitch. Go on, get out of here. I'll lock up. But call me."

"I will," I promised.

Never trust a woman who suspects you're on your way, maybe permanently, to see another woman.

No sooner was I out of the apartment than she began ransacking it. She thumbed through my address book, my mail.

"Oooohh!" she said, frustrated.

She looked up the number of the Justice Department, dialed it.

"Justice Department? Do you have someone there named Noodle? No, *Noodle!* I know it sounds silly. It's a code name." Pause. "How would I know if it's a *real* name? Does it sound like a real name? Listen, this is very important and—hey, wait a minute, don't hang up. I'm not playing a joke—"

But the operator down at Justice had cut her off.

Judy threw the phone at the wall. The cord broke just before the instrument bashed a hole in the plaster.

Bitterly, she said, "Let your fingers do the walking."

I parked my car in the short-term lot at the airport. It would cost me a fortune to bail it out later, but it was closer to the departure area.

Another car was waiting there. Naturally, I didn't see it, or its driver, Luke Martin, also known as the Bookkeeper.

His little briefcase was primed and ready. He pressed an unseen button, and a hypodermic needle slid out of the briefcase's side.

He smiled tightly and reset the spring, careful not to touch the gleaming needle point.

The Bookkeeper locked his car and followed me into the airport.

*　　　　*　　　　*

By now, my apartment was a disaster area. Judy had torn it apart, but she still hadn't found anything that would help.

"Damn it," she said, "why can't you keep a little black book like other guys?"

She gave up and went to the closet for her coat. There, she had an inspiration. She brushed her fingers along the top shelf and found Brian's picture. She took it down.

There was a business card stuck in the back and on it was written: "Noodle," and a phone number.

She rushed to the phone. It no longer worked.

She ran out, leaving the door open, an invitation to passing burglars.

At the ticket counter, I waited impatiently for the clerk to write out my ticket. He had fouled up the first one and was now laboriously filling in my name on a second.

"Don't worry, sir," he said. "Flight 904 is on time, but since you have no luggage, you'll have no trouble—"

"Stop talking and write," I said.

A slim, well-dressed man stepped up alongside me. He put his briefcase so close to me that it touched my arm.

The special telephone on Noodle's desk rang. He picked up the receiver.

185

"Noodle." He paused. "Who do you say you are? A friend of a mutual friend? Miss, I—" He paused again. "Did you call the Justice Department a few minutes ago? All right. Yes, I know your name. Slow down. How long ago did he leave?" She told him. "What flight? Yes, yes, Miss Taylor. I'll get right on it. Thank you." He hung up.

On the other end, Judy heard the click. She had called from a corner booth on the corner of St. Ann and North Rampart. She still had the photo of Brian in her hand. She was crying. She tried to stuff it into her purse, but it was too big. She put it under one arm like a book and walked aimlessly up North Rampart, avoiding the curious tourists with half a mind. Her lips were moving, but she wasn't singing.

When I felt the briefcase touch my arm, I moved away. I don't like to be crowded.

I took my ticket and started for the gate.

The slim man followed me. I only half noticed him. Maybe he was on the same flight.

I still had twelve minutes. I stopped at the magazine counter and got a newspaper.

The slim man was right behind me. He put his briefcase under one arm and fumbled for change with the other hand.

I felt its cold, hard edge against my side.

He reached for the briefcase, as if to shift its position.

The loud-speaker blared, "Passenger Kirby Grant, emergency!"

Hearing my own name startled me. I stepped closer toward the speaker.

"Passenger Kirby Grant, you are in danger. Find the nearest policeman. Do not leave the terminal. Passenger Kirby Grant—"

It repeated its message over and over.

I saw motion in the corner of my eye. The slim, well-dressed man had swung the briefcase at me, just like a bowling ball.

I ducked it.

"Hey, what the hell—"

He didn't answer. The cold, unblinking stare of his eyes was unnerving.

I didn't see the needle point protruding from the briefcase's edge, but something told me to stay away from it. I slapped at its side with my hand and his grip was broken. It skittered on the floor.

He hit me on the shoulder with a karate chop that would have killed me if it'd hit my neck where it had been aimed. I felt pain shoot down my side.

The old training came back. As I fell, I got my foot up and it caught him behind one knee. He fell backwards. I shoved a rack of books at him. By the time they had all cascaded to the floor, he was running down the corridor.

I took off after him. "Hey!" I yelled. "Stop that guy!"

In Japan, they know better. If someone wakes up and finds a burglar rummaging through his house, the cry of "Thief! Thief!" is never heard. Were it, his neighbors would all hide under their *tatami*. Instead, the victim yells, "Fire! Fire!" In that world of paper houses, fire is universally feared, and everybody rallies around to give aid.

Of course, I would have looked pretty silly running through New Orleans International Airport shouting, "Fire! Fire!"

So the crowd moved back. Nobody offered a finger of help. The guy I was chasing disappeared around a corner. I took it on one foot, like Charlie Chaplin.

I thought I saw him heading past a boarding gate.

I went through two pillars next to a security desk.

Red lights started to flash and a bell jangled.

"Hold it right there," said a security man.

"No!" I yelled, pointing. "Not me. Him! He's getting away."

He half drew his pistol.

"You freeze, mister," he warned. "And don't let me see those hands move one little bit."

The red light flashing in my eyes, the bell ringing in my ears, I said sourly, "That damned metal Playboy Club card caught me again."

EIGHT

NOBODY ever said I was smart. Instead of finding out what the hell had been going on with the well-dressed man who had attacked me, I got on my plane and flew to Atlanta, planning to call Harvey Baker when I got the chance.

Of course, I was too upset to think of it once I was on the ground. I got a cab and rushed right out to the house.

Lucille was surprised to see me.

Our conversation had an air of unreality to it.

"But you called me," I said.

"I'm sorry, Bill," she told me. "I didn't even know where you were. I still don't."

"You told me Brian had been hurt in an accident," I said grimly.

"Oh, since you're here, you might as well come in," she said. "I'll get Brian. He's already in bed, but since you've come this distance—"

And he was all right, glad to see me, sleepy-eyed,

189

puzzled—but my son, hugged close in my arms, safe.

I called Baker. It took a while to track him down. He had been on another phone trying to find me. Noodle had called him.

His first words were, "Where are you?"

I told him.

"You stay there. Don't open the door to anyone but me."

"How do I know it's you?"

"I'll ring four short times on the doorbell."

Lucille was standing behind me.

"Is it that serious?" she asked.

"I don't know," I said. "Obviously, somebody impersonated your voice. And a man tried to jump me at the airport."

She caught her breath. "Then they know where you are."

"It looks like it," I said.

She sat down. "Oh, Bill. When's it ever going to end?"

"They tell me pretty soon. Then something like this happens. You were right, Lucy. I never should have stuck my big nose in."

She touched my forehead. "No, but oddly enough, I've been quietly proud of you for it."

"That's not what you said earlier."

"Does anyone ever say what she really means?"

"I guess not," I said.

"I know it's been hard on you," she said. "I'm sorry,

Bill. About everything, not just this terrible mess because of the trial. I was hurt." She glanced at Brian, lying across the room on his stomach, watching Mission Impossible on the TV set. "And I've been unreasonable about Brian. He's been sort of a pawn between us. Well, that's over. He's your son, too. Come see him whenever you can. Or take him camping, or whatever you want—"

She stopped and looked away. I could tell she was trying not to cry.

We had a drink and watched Mission Impossible. There wasn't much to say.

The doorbell rang four times. Lucille made a move to answer it. I stopped her and went myself.

It was Baker. He slipped inside. He was unhappy with me.

"Very smart, Kirby," were his first words. "We spend a fortune hiding you out and all it takes is a couple of hours for you to blow it all to hell and gone."

"I'm sorry," I said. "I thought my boy was hurt."

"Why didn't you check with us?"

"There wasn't time. But while you're asking questions, how about asking how whoever it was who called me knew my phone number in New Orleans."

"Don't tell me—" he began, then stopped, grinning. "Oh," he said.

"I'm glad you figured it out," I said. "If their hit man knows where I am, what does it matter if you do too?"

"Well, things have changed today," he said. "Maybe it's good you're here. Because you may not have to go back."

"Why not?"

He handed me a copy of the *Atlanta Constitution*. The headline read, GANG LEADER SLAIN IN PRISON RIOT. There was a picture of Harry Cade, and under it a caption stating that he had been killed in the Federal prison that morning.

"How does Cade being dead help me?" I asked.

"The riot was phony," Baker said. "Harry's own partners had him killed. They couldn't persuade him to call off the contract on you, so they did the next best thing. They got rid of Harry."

"I'll be damned," I said.

At nine that morning, Cade had been visited by a tall, distinguished man who wore his sixty-eight years with grace. His hat was pearl gray, his suit was blue, and his ankles were actually wrapped in spats. Even the guard was startled to see him. Everyone in law enforcement recognized Vittore Steffaneli, head of Atlanta's most important Family.

Steffaneli sat carefully opposite Harry Cade and spoke quietly into the intercom telephone.

"Harry, I come to you as one old friend to another. Please, abandon this act of revenge. It is not worth the trouble it will bring to all of us."

"Shove it!" said Cade. "Vito, that fink put me in here. I said I'd get him and I will."

Steffaneli spread his hands. "What words. Anger, hostility. Toward me? Your old friend? Harry, please believe me. I want to help you."

"I'm sticking," said Harry Cade. "If you want the contract canceled, you've got to overrule me and cancel it yourself. That will take a meeting and a vote."

Steffaneli shook his head slowly. "We cannot call a meeting for such a vote. You know that. You originated the contract, and it is you who must cancel it."

"Not in a million years," said Cade.

"Please, Harry. Be reasonable."

"*You* try being reasonable! I took the goddamned fall. *I'm* rotting in here while you ride around free as you please in your big Cadillac. Well, Kirby gets his, if it costs me every dime I've got."

Quietly, the old man said, "Harry, it could cost you more than money."

"I don't care if it costs me every day of good time in this place. If I have to serve hard time, I will. The hit's still on."

Steffaneli rose. "I am sorry, my friend," he said. He hung up the phone and turned his back, so Cade did not hear him say, "Good-bye, Harry."

As he left the room, Steffaneli met the eye of a pris-

193

oner who was talking to a young woman. He gave the prisoner a slight nod.

The prisoner nodded back.

An hour later, on his way to the latrine, Harry Cade started to pass a group of inmates. They looked at him, moved toward him, surrounded him like a gray wave, and when they drifted away, Harry Cade was only a lifeless body sprawled on the concrete.

Baker had just hung up on Noodle, who had called to tell him that I was returning to Atlanta, when the phone rang again.

"Baker?" said the hoarse voice.

"Yes?"

"You heard what happened to Harry Cade this morning?"

"I heard."

"The boys want you to know that the rest of us, we got nothing against your witness, that guy Bill Kirby. It was all Harry's idea."

"What happens now that Cade is dead?"

"The contract's off."

Baker paused. Then he said, "I'm glad to hear that."

"There's only one trouble," said the hoarse voice. "We don't know where your guy is, so we don't know how to contact the button man."

"Are you asking me to give you Kirby's location?"

"It would help. Otherwise, it might take us two, three

days to track down the hit man. And who knows—during that time he might get lucky and catch up with Kirby."

"No way," said Baker. "Why should I trust you?"

"Listen, we're trying to help!" said the voice. "Okay. Play it this way. Put him under wraps for two, three days, until we catch up with Harry's man and call him off. Listen, why do you think I'm calling? We want Kirby to stay alive just as much as you do."

"How will we know when you've reached your man?"

"I'll call you again."

"You do that," said Baker.

Baker suggested that I stay in Atlanta, but I wanted to fly back to New Orleans, and I did.

Noodle met me at the gate. Judy was with him.

"Why the posse?" I asked.

"I don't want you roaming around," said Noodle. "Judy and I are taking you home and that's where you stay until that hit man has been called off."

"I'm surprised you're not taking me to jail."

Grimly, he said, "Don't think we didn't consider that."

He had a car with a driver waiting. We turned left on Williams and got onto I–10.

"I hear that Brian's all right," Judy said.

"Yeah," I said. "It was just a false alarm."

"I'm glad."

Noodle waited on the sidewalk until we'd gone up-stairs and signaled him with three buzzes on the door interlock.

Judy held out her arms.

"I was so afraid that you wouldn't come back," she said.

"It takes more than a gangster to keep me away from you," I said.

Her eyes misted.

"I wasn't thinking about gangsters," she said.

Tony D'Amato found Luke Martin early the next afternoon. They had a beer in a small West Bank bar. The juke box was already in the holiday spirit, playing "Have Yourself a Merry Little Christmas."

"I'm glad I got to you, Bookkeeper," said D'Amato. "It's all off."

"Why?"

"Just like I said. Cade is gone. Nobody else wants this Kirby clown hit, so just wipe it clean."

"What about the fifty thousand?"

"Keep it. Harry gave it to you to try. You tried."

"I was talking about the second fifty."

"There ain't no second fifty. Not now, not ever. Just forget about it, okay?"

"I took a contract," said the Bookkeeper.

"And the guy who gave it to you is dead."

Luke Martin stood up.

"Bookkeeper—" said Tony D'Amato.

"What?"

"Don't do nothing crazy."

"See you," said Luke Martin. He left.

D'Amato put a dime in the pay phone. "Operator," he said, "I want to put in a collect call."

"Collect?" said Harvey Baker in Atlanta. "You've got your nerve."

"I thought the good news would be worth it to you," D'Amato said cheerfully. "Everything's okay. I got hold of our boy. He's been called off."

"You're sure?"

"You want a polygraph?"

"Okay," said Baker. "Thanks."

NINE

JUDY and I waited for two days while Noodle checked out the underworld action in New Orleans.

He warned us, "We're not just going to take their word for it. I want to be sure there's nothing stirring."

So for two days we sat in my apartment, drinking beer and watching TV. Gus would have loved it.

There came three low taps at the door.

"That's the guard," Judy said.

I checked my watch. "Yeah, they're changing shifts now."

I opened the door. A uniformed guard was there, just seating himself in a cane-backed chair.

"Evening, folks," he said. "Everything all right?"

"Just fine," I said. "How about a drink?"

"Not on duty," he said unhappily.

"That's right," said Judy. "You're the iced tea one." He grinned. "Yes ma'am."

"Give me a few minutes," she said.

"No hurry, ma'am," he said.

I shut the door. Judy went into the kitchen and began heating some water. She slumped down over the stove and hit one small hand on its side.

"Damn!" she said.

From the door, I said, "Hang in there, baby. It can't last much longer."

"No," she said. "Of course it can't."

Out in the hall, where the guard sat reading a paperback edition of *The Winds of War,* a painter wearing white coveralls and carrying an aluminum ladder approached, whistling.

Passing in front of the guard, the painter said, "Howdy. Hot for December, ain't it?"

"You ain't just whistling 'Dixie,' " said the guard, and that was as far as he got. The painter had swung the ladder around and clobbered him against the side of the head. The guard fell out of his chair onto the heavily carpeted hallway. Quickly, the painter grabbed his wrist and dragged him into a broom closet. Inside, he hit the unconscious man three times with a leather-covered sap. Then he stripped off his coveralls and left them on the floor. Underneath, he wore a conservative business suit.

I would have recognized him instantly as the man at the airport with the slim briefcase. Luke Martin, also known as the Bookkeeper.

He tapped at our door. Twice.

Inside, Judy said, "There's our iced tea addict."

"He didn't finish the tapping," I said. We waited. No sound. "That's not the guard," I whispered.

"Maybe we missed one," she said.

I heard a scratching at the lock. Somebody was trying a key on it.

"Like hell!" I said. "Let's get out of here."

I pulled her out the French doors onto the small terrace. It connected with another one, which led to a fire escape. We crept down it in the blue of evening, trying not to make a sound.

"Look!" Judy said, pointing up at the yellow light streaming from my kitchen window. A dark shadow was moving across the ceiling. "He's inside!"

"Come on!" I yelled. I lifted her down into the back yard.

"Where's your car?" she asked, as we slipped out into the alley.

"Oh, no!" I said. "I left the keys on the dresser."

The silhouette of a man appeared in the window. We drew back into the shadows.

Maybe he hadn't been sure we were inside. Maybe he wouldn't even have seen us. But just then a car came down the alley and swept its headlights across us.

The Bookkeeper started down the fire escape.

We ran for it.

"We've got to find a phone," I said as we hurried toward the Quarter.

There was a lighted store ahead, its windows filled

with sewing notions. The cute sign read, "The Sew and Sew Shoppe." But the door was locked, and although there was an old lady inside, she took one look at us, waving and pointing at the door, and vanished into the back room.

"Maybe I should have yelled 'Fire,'" I said.

Judy gave me a puzzled look, and then we were off and running again.

On the corner of Burgundy and Conti I found a phone booth. I fumbled in my pockets for change.

"Hurry!" Judy said.

"Do you have a dime?"

"I left my purse," she said.

I pressed the coin return button. Something went clink.

"Damn it!" I said. "It's only a nickel."

"That's what a call costs in New Orleans," she said, her voice breaking.

I dropped it in. The dial tone buzzed. I hoped I remembered Noodle's private number.

I did. He answered.

"Yeah?"

"Somebody clobbered our guard and now he's chasing us," I said.

He didn't waste time. "Don't talk, Kirby. Do what I say. Get over in the Quarter. Find the most crowded place you can and stay there. Surround yourself with people. I'm on my way."

"He's coming!" Judy said, gripping my arm.

I could see a shadowy figure coming down the sidewalk. It was completely dark now.

"Run for it!" I said. I made a move toward the figure.

It came into view under a street light. It was an old man with a basket of flowers.

"Roses?" he said. "Roses for your lady?"

Judy relaxed a little. "Ohhh!" she said.

I turned to her and just then the entire side of the glass phone booth exploded under the impact of a bullet.

"Run!" I shouted, making a break down Conti. She was right alongside me.

The crowds thickened. We made our way through them, puffing for breath and looking behind. I couldn't see anyone following.

By the time we reached Bourbon Street, we were on the ragged edge of exhaustion. Surrounded by happy, laughing people, we were a drab contrast to their merriment.

"Let's get off the street," I gasped.

"Where?"

"In there," I said, pointing at a building which had once apparently been a church. Now it was prominently labeled "The Temple of Dixieland." I could hear fast, joyous music spilling out the opened double doors.

Inside we found a party atmosphere. At one end of the hall a small jazz group was jamming it for all they were worth. I think they were playing "Blues for Ja-

202

mie," but I couldn't be sure. They didn't settle on the melody line long enough for me to tell.

We must of looked like hell. The black waiter gave us a long stare before he said, "You-all want a drink, or jus' looking?"

I fumbled out a five. "Beer," I said.

Someone touched my shoulder. I whirled, ready to hit out with my fist. But it was only a middle-aged man who resembled Colonel Sanders, beard and all.

"Sorry, friend," he said. "Anybody using that extra chair?"

"No," I said. "Help yourself."

The beer came, along with four dollars change. I handed the waiter a dollar for himself. He smiled at that.

"You-all want me, just holler for Clark," he said.

"Thanks." I took a long pull at the cold Dixie beer. I looked at Judy—perspiring and hair-bedraggled.

"Sorry," I said.

"Cool it, my friend," she said. "I'm a big girl. I knew what I was signing on for."

"Well, at least we're safe in here," I said. "He wouldn't try anything in this crowd."

A quiet voice said, just behind my shoulder, "Not unless I have to."

I stiffened. Before I could turn, he added, "Don't make a move, Kirby. Or I'll drop you and fade into this mob and nobody'll even notice me."

"You're crazy," I said, trying not to let my voice

quaver. "Haven't you gotten the news? Harry Cade's dead."

"He's right," said Judy. "Cade was killed in prison."

"I took the contract," said the Bookkeeper.

"But they called it off," I said.

"I don't get called off," he said. "Walk toward the door. Slowly. Now!"

"It's all for nothing," I said. "You won't get paid a dime. Call somebody, check it out."

"Keep walking."

"I tell you, it's all a mistake."

"Mister," he said with a chuckle, "you wouldn't believe how many guys have tried to tell me that. Now move!"

I tried to catch Judy's eye, signal her to run. He wouldn't be able to chase both of us. But she was staring straight ahead.

At the door, just as we reached it, so did a marching band of slim, dark men dressed in striped shirts, red suspenders and jaunty checked pants. They were tearing into "Didn't He Ramble?" and for a second I felt a loss of contact with the man who was behind me. I dove for the outside and sensed Judy right beside me.

From behind I heard what might have been a silenced pistol shot. Or it might have been only a door slamming. Anyway, it gave wings to my feet.

We staggered down a narrow street, getting farther away from the lights and joyous uproar of the Quarter.

I gasped, "I think we lost him."

Judy didn't answer. She was running awkwardly, as if she had a stitch in her side.

We were just about out of the tourist district now. The buildings were dark, except for Christmas decorations in some of the windows.

I slowed down and listened. There wasn't any sound behind us.

"We've got to get inside somewhere," I said.

Judy stumbled. I caught her by the arm. "Easy," I said.

"I'm sorry," she choked. "I can't make it."

"Get your breath," I said.

She turned toward me, swaying.

"It isn't that," she said, and fell.

I caught her in my arms. My right hand touched something wet and slippery on her back. When I held them up, my fingers were dripping blood.

"Jesus!" I said. I pulled her to me.

"It doesn't hurt," she said weakly. "But I'm scared."

"We'll find a doctor—"

"We've got to get away," she said hoarsely. "You can't let that freak catch up. He's off his head. He'll kill us both."

I helped her along the narrow street. "Come on, baby," I said, pointing us toward the front porch of a café with a second-story metal-railed porch just like the one in *A Streetcar Named Desire*. The building was vine-crawled and gracefully old.

Its front door was locked. I knocked. A big, fat, very

suspicious black woman came to it and peered out.

"Go way," she said. "We closed."

"Please," I said. "We need help. This girl is hurt."

Still suspicious, she said, "Car wreck?"

"She's bleeding," I said.

The fat woman could see that. Reluctantly, she opened the door. I half dragged the almost unconscious Judy inside.

The fat woman protested, "Hey now, mister—this gal's been shot!"

"Call the police," I said.

"What kind of trouble you folks in?"

"Please, call the cops. We *want* them."

The woman didn't answer. She had helped Judy to a sofa and stretched her out. She tore away the back of Judy's blouse and examined the wound.

"Pore little thing," she clucked.

"Where's your phone?" I asked frantically.

"Don't have none," she said. "Nearest one's down at the corner."

I started for the front door, stopped. Someone was coming slowly down the narrow street. Without being able to see him, I knew that it was the Bookkeeper.

"How can I get up on your porch?" I whispered.

The fat woman nodded toward a stairway. I hurried to it, looking around for a weapon. There wasn't anything.

On the porch, shaded in darkness, I waited. Luke approached carefully.

I shifted my weight and the porch creaked. He started to turn his face up toward me. I leaped over the edge, trying to hit him with my shoes on the way down. That missed, but my weight toppled him and his pistol went flying.

He rolled toward it. I kicked him in the head and he let out a wild yell. I dove for the pistol, got it, and aimed it at him.

He didn't pay it the slightest bit of attention.

"You won't shoot me, Kirby."

"Don't move."

He shook his head. "You couldn't kill a man. Your kind never do."

"Just stop right there."

"Turn around and run, Kirby. That's all you know how to do."

"Don't you understand?" I said. "Harry Cade is dead. There's no *reason* any more!"

"I took a contract," he said.

"But they canceled it."

"That doesn't matter."

"You're crazy!" I said. Stupid comment. Who else but a crazy would earn a living killing other people?

He took another step. I aimed carefully and shot him in the knee.

The Bookkeeper gasped with pain and sat down.

"I warned you," I said.

White-faced, he whispered, "All right, Kirby. You've got this round."

"Just stay where you are," I said.

"Sure," he answered. "But you shot me in the wrong place. It'll heal. And what can I get for attempted assault? Two years, out in one? I underestimated you, Kirby. I won't do that next time."

"Why, for God's sake?" I yelled. "Let it be! It's over."

"Nothing's over until you're dead," he told me. And with a sinking feeling in my gut, I knew he meant what he said. As long as this man lived, my own life would be one horror of fear and hiding.

Slowly, I lifted the pistol. Its sight centered between his eyes. He stared at me—at death—without wavering.

"Drop it," said a new voice. "Now!"

I heard the click of metal against metal.

I lowered the pistol.

"On the ground," said the voice.

I let it fall.

"Now turn around."

So he'd had reinforcements in the background. I hoped Judy and the fat woman would remain inside.

Behind me, the Bookkeeper said, "Hello, Tony. You turned up just in time."

"Hi ya, Bookkeeper. So the mark was too fast for you even after all your big-mouthing."

"He won't be next time," said Luke Martin.

"No, he won't," said the other voice.

I heard a shot. I think I dove forward toward the café door. I wasn't completely sure that I hadn't been hit. Yet nothing hurt.

As I rolled to the side, there were two more shots. They were muffled, as if the gun barrel were pressing into something.

Lights started going on in nearby windows.

I heard feet running away.

Shaking, I stood up.

There was a dark bundle huddled in the street. I went over and looked down at it.

Bleeding from ears and mouth, half of his brain scattered in stringy white and red across the cobblestones, Luke Martin lay dead in the streets of New Orleans.

TEN

NOODLE came down to the *Marie II.*

"Your ex-wife called," he told me. "Your boy's on the noon plane."

"Thanks."

"She's a good woman," he said. "Are you happy in what you're doing?"

"Lucille's all right," I said. "She knows exactly what she wants. And she'll get it. I guess we just had to go through our private war, but it's over now and we can both start living again."

He shrugged. "It's your life."

"Right," I said. "Nobody promised me it would be easy."

"I still don't know why you wouldn't come down to the office."

"Noodle," I said, "it's going to be a freezing day in July the next time anybody gets me into a courthouse."

He handed me a thick folder. "Well, there's your old I.D. Driver's license, everything just like it was before."

"Nothing will ever be like it was before," I said.

Judy came out. "Who wants a beer?"

"Make it two," I said. "Noodle's suddenly off duty. He doesn't have a client any more."

She looked at the sheaf of papers in my hand.

"What's that?" she asked.

I looked down at the top card, a Georgia driver's license made out to William Kirby.

I tore it in half and dropped it overboard along with the rest of the packet.

"Nothing worth noticing," I said.

Floating in the oil slick of the harbor, the bits of paper formed a jumbled patchwork pattern. Then, slowly, they sank.